CW00391552

Beyond Tragedy
A Story of
Shanann Watts

A Novel by Vonda Knox

ISBN 979-8-7066-4167-2

Publishers Note:
Information in this book has been transcribed or paraphrased from CBI discovery documents, audio/video interviews released March 2019; Frederick Police Department, CBI, and the FBI; media interviews, FB posts, and eyewitness accounts regarding the investigation of Christopher Watts, and the events leading up to the murders of Shanann, Bella, CeCe and Nico.

Some characters and events in this book were inspired by Chief Black Kettle, Silas Soule, and events of the Sand Creek Massacre, November 29, 1864. Quote attributed to Colonel John Chivington.

Disclaimer:
The Author is expressing an interpretation of some events. All views, and opinions are solely assumed by the author.

Cover Photo
Vonda Knox, January, 2021

Dedication:

To all those who have died violent deaths,
& now speak from the stars, with the voices of
angels.

"Professor, is this all real,
or is it just happening inside my head?
Of course it's happening
inside your head Harry.
Why should that mean that it's not real?"

Harry Potter & the Deathly Hallows
J.K. Rowling

Special Thanks:
Rose, Virgil, Don, & R.M., thank you for your
attentive listening skills, your exuberant
support, and your honest feedback.

Introduction

Each morning I rolled out of bed, washed my face, and stumbled directly to the coffee pot. While drinking my first cup of morning energy I snuggled up with the TV remote. "My camera," were the first words of the new day. I waited for the programing of the porch motion sensor camera to reveal what had been looming in the driveway in the late hours of the night, or the early hours of the morning. For five long months I was not disappointed. An unexplainable orb, usually the size of a large basketball, woke the silent camera with a hazy light, swaying in from unexpected directions, and crossing the path of the blue truck parked in the driveway. Along with several cynics in the house, and the curious neighbors, we explored every possible, logical, explanation for the orbs; flashlights, drones, street lights, neighbors, strangers. Given the random direction the orbs moved, the varying times they occurred, and the sheer number of nights they were observed, we concluded that it would take a pretty determined, perhaps very bored person to mount such an elaborate ruse. There was no logical explanation!

The house next door, the Watt's house, has seen countless inquisitive visitors. Pictures, videos, documentaries, podcasts and endless speculation saturate the internet and the news outlets. People drive across state lines, or across the country, motivated by a need to connect with Shanann and the kids, hoping the house will offer some kind of closure or understanding. They stand on the front lawn, look in the windows, and take selfies. Some just want to see where a murder occurred, many are profoundly saddened. They wipe back tears, cry openly, or say a little prayer. They light candles, and leave stuffed toys and flowers. The story itself has reached around the world. Curiosity, sadness, disbelief, anger, quite possibly every emotion one can think of, has been linked to this location and this tragic story. Whatever one thinks about energy and how it works, the house on Saratoga Trail in Frederick, Colorado, has been inundated with it.

Over the last two years, I quite frequently felt Shanann and her children. I have upon occasion caught a glimpse of the girls, with their sweet little smiles, running through the halls of my home. I heard Shanann whispering in my room at night and I met her in my dreams. I began having respectful conversations with her. I meditated, burned sage, lit candles, and said prayers. I began hearing a dialogue, a narrative was coming through, and a story emerging. Images were appearing in my dreams. Much to my surprise, I met characters I did not expect, yet their presence made perfect sense to me. They were here long before anyone in this neighborhood.

I have often felt the presence of those who have passed, on one level or another. There are untold interpretations and perceptions of the afterlife. Is communication between realms possible? Is this only in my mind? Who is to say? I am sharing my experience, and the story that has come to me. You, as a reader, have the right, and the responsibility of formulating your own opinion.

Chapter One

Shanann opened her eyes. She could barely make out the shadowy ceiling, and her bedroom felt colder than usual. Even in the middle of August the evenings always seemed to cool down in Colorado, a far cry from the humidity and the heat she had known while living in North Carolina. The six-week vacation she and the girls had just spent with her parents distinctively refreshed her memory. Even though it was ridiculously hot, it was good to be with her mom, dad, and her brother Frankie. This would be a working vacation, but Shanann also planned some much needed down time with her family and her in-laws. Her business was thriving, and she was definitely feeling her third pregnancy. She was exhausted at times, and always seemed hungry. Her usually supportive husband, Chris, seemed to have forgotten his role while she and the girls were in North Carolina. He was distant when he joined them the fifth week. No kiss at the airport, what? He couldn't keep his hands off of her before she and the girls had left.

Vacations end and they were all finally home. After one short business trip to Arizona with her friend Nickole, she would settle in and deal with whatever was going on with her husband. Trying to figure out what was in Chris's mind launched Shanann into a full panic. *Oh my God, what a terrible nightmare!* Shanann was trembling and afraid to get out of the bed. She felt dizzy and her throat was dry. Her craving for a drink of water was urgent and all-consuming. She had to get up, her throat was burning. She overcame her fear and cautiously crept from the bed. The room seemed hazy and oddly silent as she made her way into the bathroom.

The light was dim, and it took her a minute to focus well enough to see herself in the mirror. She was shocked at her image. Her eyes were completely bloodshot, and there was a small dark bruise on the right side of her neck. Suddenly, a memory came crashing in with a vengeance. *He is on top of me! Chris is on top of me! Why can't I move? You're going to hurt the baby! Get your hands off my neck! Why am I so weak? This isn't happening. You can't do this! You won't do this!* Shanann was searching for her breath, for enough air to fill her lungs. *Get off of me so I can breathe.* Chris was so aggressive, and something horrible had happened, but she couldn't remember exactly what it was. Her thoughts immediately shifted to the girls. *Where are Bella and CeCe?* Shanann bolted from the bathroom and ran to their bedrooms. The bed covers revealed that the girls had been sleeping, but they weren't there. *Bella, CeCe, are you hiding from mommy? Chris, where is Chris? Is his truck here? Where are my girls?* Shanann started down the stairs. On the third step she tripped, landed on her back, and slid down the staircase like a bag of laundry. Shanann jumped up and immediately went to the front porch. Chris's truck was gone. He had already left for work. *Why did he take the girls? This is so confusing! Maybe they are hiding the garage or on the driveway?*

Shanann went through the garage, and over to the neighbor's driveway calling for the girls. "Bella, CeCe, mommy is worried. If you are playing you need to come out and see me now."

Suddenly, a vaguely familiar voice called her name. It was coming from inside the house, from the kitchen. *Who is calling my name?* Shanann followed the voice. Her grandmother was standing in the kitchen by the sliding glass doors that opened to the back porch.

"Hi, honey. Oh, my sweet girl, you have grown into such a beautiful woman."

"Gran, what are you doing here?"

Shanann was surprised to see her grandmother. She hadn't seen her for years, since... She looked radiant, and the entire kitchen smelled like flowers. The fragrance was intoxicating. Shanann suddenly longed to touch it, taste it, to bathe in it. As delightful as the smell was, it dimmed in comparison to the light that flooded into the kitchen. The translucent hues of dancing light were mesmerizing. It was so vivid. Shanann squinted in the brilliance.

"Beautiful, isn't it?" It was Gran's voice, but her lips didn't move. They were smiling with the joy that only comes from addressing a precious grandchild.

Shanann was suddenly overcome with warmth and peace. The light was engulfing her, and she was filled with an insatiable desire to be in the light, to be part of it, to be the light. Shanann's attention was drawn from the intense desire to experience it fully when she heard a cry. She looked over and saw that her grandmother was holding a baby. A mother never forgets the first sound of her newborn child.

"Shan, honey, this is Nico. He is longing to meet you." Gran spoke with unfathomable tenderness. Shanann was overwhelmed with joy and excitement.

"Oh my God, he looks just like Frankie," Shanann exclaimed, as she took her lovely boy from the arms of her grandmother. His skin felt velvet-soft as she kissed his tiny forehead and his small fingers grasped her forefinger.

"Can I see the baby, mommy?" a small voice asked. CeCe was reaching for her baby brother.

"Thank God, CeCe, you are here with mommy! I was so worried about you." Shanann showed CeCe her new baby brother. She was overcome with uncontrollable love for her children. Nico's tiny little nose wriggled as he yawned.

"We can go now, Shanann," Gran whispered softly. "We can all go to the light. It is so peaceful in the open meadows. You and the babies have such had a hard time."

Shanann nodded in acknowledgment. She wanted to go to the light with Gran. She was ready. A cold breeze suddenly entered from the living room. Shanann felt a gripping chill run down her spine. "Wait, where is Bella?" Shanann asked.

"Bella has decided not to join us yet, but I'm sure she is fine," Gran explained.

"What do you mean? She is a four year old. She needs to be here with me. Where is she?" Shanann asked frantically.

"I am sure she is fine," Gran repeated.

"I don't understand. Why can't Bella come with us?" Shanann asked.

"She can come and join us any time. It is up to her to decide when the time is right. No one can make that decision for her," Gran, explained.

"So she is out there all alone? Oh my God!" Shanann cried.

"She isn't alone. No one is alone. She will come to us when she is ready."

"Gran, I can't go." Shanann looked at her very happy children and realized that she could not possibly leave without Bella, no matter what.

Gran knew the granddaughter she loved so deeply had made up her mind. "I understand," she said gently.

"Everyone decides when the time is right," Shanann repeated what Gran had said, reassuring herself. "Will you take my babies with you, Gran?"

"Of course dear. Don't worry, they won't even know you are gone. Time works differently here."

Shanann reached over and kissed her sleeping baby boy. She reached down and gave CeCe a big hug. "I love you so much honey. I am going to find Bella so she can be with us."

CeCe's face lit up and her smile filled the room. Shanann felt unconditional love and acceptance as her grandmother took her two children, and walked into the fragrance and the beautiful light. She knew they would be perfectly safe and happy. Shanann was so grateful for Gran. She had always felt her love, even after she passed all those years ago.

When Gran and the kids went out the back door, the room suddenly became chilly. The feeling of perfect acceptance was replaced with a fierce, compelling need to protect her child, her Bella. Shanann's clarity left with Gran and her children. She was suddenly foggy about Chris and everything that had happened. Events spilled into one another. She was having a hard time remembering the order, the details. Memories drifted in and out, but she knew one thing for certain, she needed to find her daughter. Nothing and no one would stand in her way! Fear and anxiety did not have a place in her resolve. Her determination dug deeply into the roots of her existence, deep into the sacred space where her body had grown her child; the place where they had bonded beyond time and space; the moment they agreed to journey into the physical world together and be joined by a bond of love. They were mother and daughter.

Shanann explored the silent house; all of the rooms, closets, cupboards, small spaces, anywhere a small child of four might be hiding. In her heart, she knew her daughter was not in the house, but her motherly instincts were too strong not to comply. *I need to find my daughter and I don't know how to do this.* She thought about calling her friends, but she couldn't remember their numbers. *Where is my phone?* Shanann walked out the front door and stood on the porch. This was her home. She brought her babies here when they were first born. She watched them grow into little girls, frustrating her, challenging her, filling her heart with tremendous joy. *Bella, where are you? Thank God Gran has CeCe and Nico. Bella isn't alone! Gran told me that.* Suddenly, Shanann wondered why she was alone. The thought was like a whisper in her mind. Much to her surprise, a man was standing on her front lawn facing away from her. Shanann noticed the long dark braid centered in the middle of his back and a small circle of smoke dancing around his head. He slowly and deliberately moved his hands in front of his face, directing the smoke above him, and then down and toward his body. Shanann knew he was aware of her presence, but he continued directing the smoke and chanting something quietly. She could hear his words, but she didn't understand them. The man stretched his arms out to his sides and raised his palms to the sky as if expecting something to fill his hands. The smoke began to subside as he turned to look at her. Shanann was totally enthralled. His vest was tied in the front in several places, and he wasn't wearing a shirt underneath. His loose-fitting beige pants were tied on the sides, and Shanann thought they might be made of some sort of animal skin, deer maybe? Her thoughts suddenly drifted off; *a trip to the Denver Zoo with the girls; a doe and a fawn. Oh, those giggles!* Shanann returned her thoughts to the man in front of her. Three feathers stood proudly in his braid. They looked soft yet strong, probably eagle feathers she guessed. Shanann could smell the smoke as she met the gaze in his dark brown eyes. She instinctively knew he was burning sage and conducting some kind of a prayer, or ritual.

As if listening to her thoughts, he began speaking, "I am praying for my people, for the ones who are still wandering this plain."

Shanann was mesmerized by the soothing, yet strong nature of his voice. She immediately felt a great wave of peace.

"I am looking for my daughter. Have you seen a little girl about this tall?" she asked, holding her hand out to show him Bella's height.

He looked at her intently, "Who is your daughter?"

Shan answered, "Bella, her name is Bella."

"No, who is she?"

Shanann thought for a second. "She is calm and observant. Her smile lights up the room and she takes care of everyone."

A slight smile crossed his lips, "Yes, I know your child. She used to see me when she was very small. She sensed my presence when no one else did."

Shanann paused as if in a lost moment, "I remember. We wondered what she was responding to. That was you?"

"Your child is very perceptive. She can see between the worlds of time and place."

"My mother knows things as well. Her faith is strong," Shanann explained. *Maybe it's genetic.* "I'm Shanann," she offered a little wave as she introduced herself.

"I am Speaks With Stars."

"Speaks With Stars," Shanann repeated his name. It slid off of her tongue, as if it were liquid silver. "It's beautiful."

Speaks With Stars smiled slightly before he spoke, "It wasn't my first name. It was given to me by my grandmother when I was your daughter's age. My first name was Fire Starter. As a toddler, I was always attracted to fire. When the other children were stumbling about playing, I would collect sticks and stack them for the fire. At night I would sit by the flames for hours and gaze at the stars. One night the fire went out and my father came and poked me with a long stick. 'If you are going to sit here, do your job. Put more wood on that fire,' he said. My grandmother heard the commotion and came out. She was a very wise woman and a healer. 'This boy is not a fire starter. His job is to speak with the stars,' she declared. She went back to her teepee without another word. The next day my father told the tribe my new name."

Shanann was intrigued by his story, and for one moment she was not consumed with her desire to find Bella. The moment passed, however, and her worry intensified as if she had suddenly lost not moments, but days. She was very confused, but focused on her goal. "Do you know where my daughter is? Have you seen her?"

"I have not seen your Bella, yet I sense that she is looking for something. You may not find her until she has found it," Speaks With Stars answered directly.

"I don't understand. My other kids are with my Gran. She came to get them and she took them to a safe place."

"Your grandmother is a wise woman!"

Shanann nodded and continued, "They were happy to go with her." Shanann remembered the delight on CeCe's face and the beautiful baby boy that Gran carried as she left. Shanann hesitated as if she had just realized how interesting the situation was. Her thoughts drifted in and out as if in a dream. She wandered in her own mind, noticing that her senses were on high alert. She could feel the crispness of the cool air, even though she knew it was summer. She could smell the sage and the newly cut grass. Fragrance from the flowers in the neighbor's yard drifted through the air. When she looked into Speaks with Stars' eyes, she saw more than a deep rich brown. She could see Him, and in some odd way she occasionally saw her own reflection. At moments, their thoughts merged and she could tell what he was thinking. He was doing the same thing with her, but he was much better at it.

Speaks With Stars looked directly at Shanann. He confirmed their connection with a slight smile.

She was mesmerized by their deep connection, but at the same time wondered why he was standing on her front lawn in Frederick, Colorado.

Speaks With Stars intuitively offered her an explanation. "My people were here many years ago. There was a battle southeast in a land near the Sand Creek. Many people were killed without mercy. They died violently and suddenly. They missed their families and didn't understand what happened to them. Some still wander, looking for answers."

Shanann looked deeply into his eyes. "Are you a guide? Do you show them the way?" she asked softly.

His eyes were filled with compassion and his words were tender, "Everyone must find their own way. I am here to let them know they are not alone."

"Those people by the Sand Creek, did they figure out what happened to them, who murdered them?" Shanann asked intently.

"Yes, the truth comes out," he assured her.

Shanann suddenly seemed distracted. "I am going in the house now to look for Bella." She started walking to the door, turned, and looked at Speaks With Stars. "If you see my Bella, please let me know. It was nice meeting you."

Speaks With Stars felt a very deep pang of sympathy for Shanann. He could sense her confusion and the heaviness in her heart. He watched her go into the house. Speaks With Stars re-lit his sage and started a small fire in the middle of the lawn, which was somehow now a dirt mound surrounded by rocks. A small teepee stood nearby. Baskets filled with berries sat next to the fire pit. He took the sage and carefully blew the smoke in each direction. East, north, west, and south towards Shanann's house. He picked up a small drum and begin beating it as he chanted the prayers of the elders. The fire in the pit grew larger, and the rhythm took on a life of its own. Soon, the flames of the fire joined in the ritual, dancing and crackling, to the beat of his drum. Speaks With Stars banged the instrument loudly and his song grew more intense. The deep compassion he felt for Shanann and the small child who saw him through time, strengthened the sound.

Chapter 2

Shanann isn't answering her phone. Nickole was officially in a state of panic now. The trip to Arizona had been rough. Shan wasn't her happy, positive self. It was un-nerving! This is something beyond the discomfort of pregnancy. Chis was being weird and Shanann was clearly upset. *She isn't answering the phone. The house is dead silent. Where is she? Why isn't she answering her phone? Where are the police? Something is so wrong. Thank God the police are here.*

"How are you doing? You're Nickole? What's going on?" Office Coonrod of the Frederick police department asked.

Nickole began to explain to the officer, "My friend and I were out of town for a business trip this weekend. I dropped her off at 2:00 this morning. She is fifteen weeks pregnant and she wasn't feeling well. Shanann had a doctor's appointment at 9:00, and I told her to reach out, if she needed me to take her. She has two little girls and she was very distraught over the weekend, not eating or drinking normally. We kept trying to force her, because she is pregnant. She and her husband are supposedly going to separate, but she didn't know that. Shan thought they were just having issues. Chris just told me that today. I called him and asked if he had talked to Shanann, or heard from her this morning, because I couldn't get a hold of her. I called. I texted. Her car is in the garage. The shoes she wears every single day are right at the front door."

"She only has one vehicle?" Office Coonrod asked.

"They only have the one car and the work truck. Chris said Shanann took the girls and went on a play date, but they are only four and three. If she went on a play date why wouldn't she take the car? They are both in car seats. She had a doctor's appointment at 9:00 and she didn't go to her appointment." Nickole repeated the information as she continued going over and over all of the details in her mind. *This doesn't make sense.*

"No answer on the phone, and her husband's on his way?" Officer Coonrod asked.

"Supposedly, but he said that thirty minutes ago, and when I called again, he said he was forty-five-minutes out. I know the combination to the front door but there is a lock on the inside," Nickole explained.

"What about the garage door?"

"I don't have that code."

"Would you mind calling her husband to see if we can get a pass code, and see if he'll give me permission to go in? I'm just going to check the back. I want to look at all of the windows to see if anything is out of place." Officer Coonrod walked around the house checking all of the windows and lowering himself into the window wells. There was no sign of movement, no noise. Everything was in order. Officer Coonrod climbed the deck stairs. He saw his solitary reflection in the sliding glass door as he knocked loudly. He noticed the next door neighbor who was standing on his porch with his dogs. The houses were close to one another, and it wasn't difficult to carry on a conversation from one porch to the other.

"How you doing?" Officer Coonrod asked. "Have you seen your neighbors today?"

"No, what's going on?" Nate responded with curiosity.

"We're just trying to get in touch with her. She wasn't feeling too good, and she's pregnant. They are just concerned. You didn't see her today, outside or anything?"

"No, I know he works in the oil fields. I haven't seen her, but that's pretty normal. I think she might be diabetic. She has something going on with her blood sugar levels," Nate offered.

"Oh, does she?" The idea that Shanann had some kind of serious illness was even more troubling. Officer Coonrod thanked Nate and proceeded with even more urgent deliberation. He was on high alert as he went over all of the possible scenarios. *People don't disappear, poof! A pregnant woman and two little girls. Maybe the grandparents came to pick them up. Maybe Shanann's phone is dead. Fourth amendment; right to the house, I need permission to go in. If the kids answered, I could go in.* Officer Coonrod knocked loudly again. "Come on, answer the door. Shit! How am I going to get in here?" *Okay, plan B. I have to wait for Chris.*

Nothing seemed out of place in the back yard. The lush green grass was meticulously mown. The festive yellow hood on the swing set, and the pink plastic lawn mower were silent. The colorful cushions on the wrought iron chairs, resting on the deck, seemed inviting, and the large square fire-pit table glimmered in the sunlight. The view off the back porch was nothing short of gorgeous. The majestic Colorado Mountains and the soft billowy clouds knew nothing of a mishap. Officer Coonrod slowly walked back to the front of the house. He knocked on the front door and looked into the silent living room. Nickole was in the driveway talking on the phone with Shanann's mom, Sandy. Both women were going back and forth, trying to fit the pieces together. "What play date, what friend, why is the car in the garage?"

"What is Chris's phone number?" Officer Coonrod moved quickly to plan B. Nickole gave him the number and he dialed immediately.

She listened anxiously.

"Hey Chris, Officer Coonrod, Frederick Police Department. Pretty Good. So do you have any idea where your wife is? My concern is that her car is here and they are saying she has health issues. I don't know if she is upstairs and can't respond. How far out are you? Okay, thanks!" Officer Coonrod spoke loudly into his voice recorder, "This female has health issues; unknown if she is home; husband is five minutes away." Waiting for Chris, officer Coonrod continued peeking into the living room through the windows. He asked for Shanann's phone number and tried to call her. *If she is in the house, I may be able to hear the phone ring.* Nothing. He yelled loudly, "Shanann are you home?" A tiny bark broke the silence as the family dog responded with defiance. "Police department! If anyone is inside, make yourself known."

Chris finally pulled up in his work truck. He jumped out of the vehicle and quickly made his way to shake the officer's hand. After confirming his identity, he went directly to the garage door and entered the code. Shanann's car was parked in the garage.

"Is this the only vehicle she has? The only one she would drive?" Officer Coonrod inquired.

Chris answered in the affirmative. He opened the passenger door to the car as if looking for something. He quickly left the garage and entered his home.

Nate, who had joined Nickole in the front yard, revealed that he had a motion sensor camera on the front porch of his house.

"Yeah, my camera picked up motion about 2:00 a.m., Nate offered.

"That was me," Nickole declared. "That's when I dropped Shanann off."

"Can you see motion during the day?" Officer Coonrod asked.

"Yeah, I can go look again." Nate offered.

"Would you mind?"

Nate took off, and Nickole continued speaking to Sandy, who was listening intently from North Carolina. Nickole asked the officer if she could join Chris in the house.

"I mean it's up to him. It's his house," Officer Coonrod replied.

"Nickole, I give you permission to go into my daughter's house." Sandy's directive was heard loudly from the speaker on Nickole's phone.

"Mind if I come in Chris?" Officer Coonrod asked. Chris gave his permission and they entered the home. The very large house was well organized and spotlessly clean. If something were out of place it would have been obvious. Chris moved from room to room intently looking for something.

"You checked upstairs, and she's not there? I just want to make sure she isn't passed out somewhere. Is she diabetic? Do you mind if I look around?" Officer Coonrod asked.

The sudden excitement, and the strangers in the house, prompted a barking frenzy from the Watts' family dog. "You're fine Dieter," Chris assured the confused dog as he ushered him out the back door onto the porch.

With flashlight in hand, Officer Coonrod went upstairs and meticulously inspected each room. He occasionally caught a glimpse of Chris, who seemed to be doing the same. Everything was orderly and in its proper place. Officer Coonrod went down into the basement. Once again he saw that everything was tidy, and organized. *Everything seems perfect! No sign of a struggle or an intruder.* Officer Coonrod went back upstairs. *There is no sign of Shanann or the girls. There is no sign of any kind of disruption in this home, weird!*

Chris confirmed what they all expected, "She's not at home."

Officer Coonrod inquired, "Any friends she might be with?"

Chris walked back and forth, only pausing briefly to answer the officer's questions. He calmly mentioned a couple of names.

"I guess her parents are out of state?" Officer Coonrod asked.

"Yeah, they are across the country in North Carolina." Chris continued, "All of the girl's blankets are gone. The blankets they sleep with. They don't go anywhere without them." Chris sounded concerned.

"Nothing else appears to be missing, stuff you might take for a quick trip?"
Officer Coonrod looked closely in the girl's room hoping for something, any clue.

Chris walked into the upstairs hall. He pointed to the staircase ledge. "Her phone's here."

"Her phone's here?" Nickole immediately panicked.

"Does she work?" Officer Coonrod asked.

"Yes, she works from home," Nickole and Chris chimed in together.

Chris picked up the phone, "Yep, this is her lifeline." Chris looked intently at Shanann's phone. He asked Nickole if she knew the pass code.

"I don't know the code. Try the baby's due date." Nickole was pacing back and forth. *I was just with you Shan. I dropped you off hours ago? Where are you?* Nickole had called everyone she could think of.

Chris continued looking through the different numbers. He was chewing on his lip as he stared at Shanann's phone, her lifeline."

Officer Coonrod inquired, "What does she do for work?"

"She works for a direct sales company, Le-Vel," Chris responded.

"How often does her blood sugar drop?" Officer Coonrod asked.

"She was having some issues this weekend," Nickole answered.

"But she doesn't pass out, or anything?" Officer Coonrod inquired.

Chewing his lip, speaking rapidly, and motioning with his hands, Chris offered a timeline, and shared personal details with the police officer standing in his home. "No, she used to, but that was a long time ago after she was in a car wreck. She takes medicine for her migraines, and she took more this month than she ever has before, because of the humidity in North Carolina where she was vacationing for six weeks. We got back Monday or Tuesday, and then she flew to Arizona Friday morning. She got back last night about 2:00 in the morning. Her flight was delayed. She left the airport about 11:00 and got here at 2:00 a.m., and then I went to work this morning about 5:15."

"What do you do?" Officer Coonrod asked.

"I work oil and gas."

"What do you do for them?"

"Operator."

"Long days then?"

"Yeah, I ah, yeah." Chris smiled and shrugged, relieved at the small talk. Chris rocked back and forth as he and Nickole continued to try and access Shanann's phone.

"Can you look at your doorbell camera to see if she left on the play date? You said that she went on a play date?" Nickole asked.

"That's what she told me." Chris continued to look at Shanann's phone. Holding it firmly in his hands it seemed to stabilize him in the surreal situation.

"Where do the kids go to school?" Officer Coonrod asked.

Chris answered the question without looking up.

"Sandy wants to talk to you." Nickole handed Chris her phone and his frantic mother-in-law.

"Yeah, she went to a friend's house," Chris explained. "That's what she told me. I have no clue why she didn't take her phone. The camera on the front door? Yeah, I can take a look, but it is so random. It has been going off and on lately. It false tripped, told me it was open when I got here. No, it doesn't make any sense at all. I don't know where Shanann and the kids are," Chris continued to pace while absorbing the panic from his mother-in-law on the other end of the phone line. Sandy was direct in her questioning.

"Nate, the next door neighbor, says no one left the house during the day," Nickole reported.

"What's that?" Chris turned and asked her, happy for the interruption.

"Your neighbor, he has a camera. He said no one left the house during the day. He says there was some movement about 2:00 a.m. when I dropped Shanann off."

Chris ended the conversation with his distraught mother-in-law, and assured her that he would call her the minute he knew something. He continued starring into the phone. His jaw was set and he showed no interest in the fact that the neighbor's camera might have information about his missing wife and daughters.

"Dispatch 91, you can cancel medical at this stage," Officer Coonrod phoned in.

Chris continued to stare into his phone as if looking for some mysterious answer.

"What time did you leave for work?" Officer Coonrod asked.

"About 5:50 this morning."

"Was Shanann here when you left this morning?" The officer's voice was stern.

"Yeah, she was right in the bedroom." Chris looked to the bedroom and then back at his phone, his best distraction.

"Does she usually watch the kids, or do you have daycare watch them?"

Chris looked up long enough to answer, "She usually watches the kids at the house."

Nickole called from downstairs, "Could she be at the pool?"

"We have a pool down at the clubhouse," Chris explained to Officer Coonrod. "I can run down there and check." Chris seemed anxious to be away from the questions.

"You guys have any kind of issues? Marital issues or, anything?" Officer Coonrod asked.

Chris answered quietly, "We are going through a separation."

"You guys file anything yet, or you just talk about it?"

"No, I want to sell the house."

"And how's that going, civil for the most part?" Officer Coonrod inquired.

Chris shrugged slightly and offered a little smile before returning his gaze to the phone, proceeding with his determined search.

"Does your wife go to the pool often?"

"It just depends. On a hot day like today, I would say no."

Chris suddenly announced, "It says at 5:27 a.m. the garage overhead door was open and never shut." He seemed to be revealing the magical message that he had been studiously searching for.

"What time did you leave?" Nickole asked.

"At 5:27, I pulled away and shut the door. It never shut," Chris declared.

"It was shut when I got here," Nickole stated, shutting down his idea with a shrug.

"It was closed? Well then the sensor is tripping out, which happened before. I had to replace it two weeks ago." Chris quickly jumped out of his idea and back into complacency.

"Does she do her work from a laptop, or just from her phone?" Officer Coonrod asked.

Once again Nickole and Chris answered in unison, "She only uses her phone."

"What about the bank account?" Nickole inquired.

"I already tried, but her log-in is different than mine."

"It's not a joint account"? Officer Coonrod asked.

"It's a joint account, but she controls all of it. It kind of goes back in the day. She handles all of that. I have the apps on my phone, but I don't have her log-in to get into it."

"What days does she work?" Officer Coonrod asked.

"Every day, always!" Chris replied quickly.

"What was the name of the company again?"

"Le-Vel," Chris answered, showing slight irritation.

"Where are they located?"

"They don't really have an office," Chris responded.

"Does she have someone she reports to though?"

"She has her leaders, but they are in the eastern part of the country." Chris named off a few of the Le-Vel employees. He looked down, slightly biting his lip, clearly distressed. Officer Coonrod and Chris entered the master bedroom. The bedding had been removed from the enormous four post bed. A steady hum could be heard from the ceiling fan. Chris commented that he had found Shanann's wedding ring sitting on the night stand.

"There wasn't a note near the ring?" Officer Coonrod asked. "Any of her clothes missing, anything like that? It doesn't look like she packed a bag or anything?"

The clothes, the ring, the lovely flowers by the bathtub, the pictures on the walls, all present and accounted for. The only thing missing was the woman who put it all together, the woman who drew the bath, decorated the home, wore the ring and filled the closet.

Officer Coonrod persisted, "Did she tell you anything about leaving, or moving out?"

"Not moving out," Chris quickly answered. For the first time he looked directly at Officer Coonrod. "The last time I talked to her, she said she was going to take the kids to a friend's house, and that's where she was going to be. I texted her today. I never heard anything. The car is here unless someone came and picked her up. But the people that I know; no one has seen her. No one has heard from her." He spoke the words slowly and deliberately as if to challenge the officer's questions. *This is what I am saying. This is my story. Can't you just leave it alone?*

"Definitely an odd one," Officer Coonrod's statement snapped Chris back from his moment of defiance.

"I don't know what to do. Should I drive around and look for her, you know on a route where she might be?" Chris asked in a passive voice?

"Where does she normally go?"

"Maybe by the kid's school, by the neighbors down the street, the only routes I know she might take," Chris rationalized.

"Does she go to the neighbor's frequently?"

"Not much, but, do you think it's smart to drive around and look for her?"

"Obviously not. You don't know what car she would be in," Officer Coonrod stated.

Nickole and Chris continued to call everyone they could think of, anyone who might know where Shanann and the girls were.

"I have my detective coming. This is an odd one. He may have you call the bank."

Officer Coonrod asked Chris about work, "How long have you been in the oil field?"

"Since 2015. I worked at two different companies. Before that, I worked on cars for eleven years."

"Do you like it?"

"I love the fact that I don't have carpal tunnel in my wrist. That's why I quit. It was destroying my body. Oil fields are less repetitive, and it gives me time with the kids. I used to be eight days on and then eight days off, but now I'm on a five-two shift. It gives me more time with the kids and gives her some time off."

"Does she have any other medical conditions?"

"Lupus. We thought she had R.A. She took a lot of medications and had flare ups before she moved here in 2012."

"Any medication changes or behavioral changes? Anything like that recently?"

"No, nothing like that," Chris assured.

While waiting for the detectives, Nickole, Chris, and Officer Coonrod decided to go next door to Nate's house and watch the video from the motion camera that was mounted on the porch. The living room was large, yet the high vaulted ceilings weren't quite tall enough to hold the anticipation that filled the room.

Nate spoke into his TV remote, "My camera."

Officer Coonrod, Nickole, and Chris waited anxiously to see what might be revealed on the TV screen. The ominous view suddenly appeared. Nate's truck was in the forefront of the shot, and behind the tree, Chris's truck could be seen backing into the driveway. Even with a tree between the two houses it was clear that Chris made several trips from the house to the truck. Attention was directed at the video with a sense of urgency as they watched Chris on the recording. Everyone in the room was laser focused, except Chris, who kept looking down at his phone. Nate and officer

Coonrod searched closely for clues, any small sign that Shanann had left the house. Did someone pick her up, any unusual cars parked, anyone drive away, anything?

After quickly glancing at the video, Chris once again turned his eyes urgently to his phone.

"Is the camera continuous, or is it motion sensitive?" Officer Coonrod asked.

"Its motion," Nate answered. "It picks up cars coming from each direction." Nate continued to explain what he had seen on the video as Nickole and Officer Coonrod watched with him.

Chris looked up abruptly and offered an explanation as to why he had backed his truck into the driveway. "I didn't want to lug everything out there, all the tools I had to bring in."

As the others looked diligently at the video, hoping for some clue, Chris glanced outside, towards the front door. His sunglasses were perched on top of his head as he moved nervously from side to side. He linked his fingers behind his head, lightly chewed his lip, and swayed back and forth, as he watched himself loading the truck. Once again, he told the officer everything that he had loaded into the truck, as if repeating it, two or three times, somehow made it more significant.

Chris turned to the officer, "What else can I do?" His hands were still linked behind his head, his face was pale, and fraught with tension. He was still chewing his lip.

"My detective just showed up, and he'll probably want to talk to you. He might want you to call the bank and see if there is any activity."

Nate was intently watching every second of the video. "If there is any sort of motion out there this camera would have caught it," Nate explained while pointing to the TV.

Chris replied, "We had some issues the other week, like, people were stealing stuff out of garages, and stuff like that, like, they were using screw drivers to jimmy..." Chris's explanations were disorderly as he pointed to the small area on the video that revealed his truck and a vague image of himself.

"If there was anything right in this area, it should have picked it up," Nate assured him. "It will pick up anything coming down the street, this way, and the other way."

"Even with that tree there?" Chris quickly asked.

"Oh, yeah," Nate proceeded to show Chris another video that captured the view they were referring to. "See what I'm saying. It picks up everything."

Officer Coonrod told Chris that his detective had arrived and was next door.

"Do you want me to go?" Chris quickly asked, pointing to the door, seemingly anxious to escape the room and the situation.

Office Coonrod indicated that he wanted Chris to stay. They both returned their attention to the TV, as Nate explained, in detail, every view from the camera lens. "It would have caught her, or anyone walking out of your house." He scrolled through the many clips and revealed the full range of the camera.

Chris turned, continued swaying, and glanced back at the TV. Nate pushed the remote button so they could see the next frame. The view of the driveway was suddenly replaced by a TV commercial. Nate spoke directly into the remote, trying to retrieve the clips they were reviewing. "My camera," he repeated, insistently. The screen did not go back into review mode, instead, an unborn fetus suddenly appeared on the screen. The small body sat silently in a heart shaped womb. Chris stared at the image, then turned to Officer Coonrod. Any color he had left in his face had suddenly disappeared, "She's pregnant as well," he stated.

Officer Coonrod didn't miss a beat, "How far along?"

"Fourteen, fifteen weeks," Chris responded. A look of intense annoyance, almost anger, masked Chris's passive demeanor for only a fraction of a second. After Chris briefly disclosed that his wife was pregnant with their unborn child; an atomic explosion appeared on the TV screen; a beautiful woman turned into a skeleton, and hands reached up out of black oil as they grasped a human skull. Chris had turned his back, and didn't see the images. Nate was busy with the remote trying to get the clips back. The gruesome, strange, images went unnoticed by Officer Coonrod, and Nickole had left the room. The conversation continued without anyone hearing the faint sound of drumming and chanting, and no one seemed to notice the smell of burning sage.

"That's why her friends were so concerned about her low blood sugar," Chris offered, regarding his pregnant wife. They continued looking at different clips.

"Did you look around to see if anything was missing at your house?" Nate asked.

"Her wedding ring was still on the night stand."

Nate continued to view the camera and asked, "So, Nickole dropped her off at one something in the morning right?"

"My doorbell camera says 1:48," Chris responded.

Nate found the clip of Nickole driving away.

"The camera didn't pick up Shanann going into the house?" Officer Coonrod asked.

"It didn't," Nate answered, navigating to the view of Chris.

"It picked up Chris walking right here," Nate pointed to the screen. "But, it didn't pick up Shanann leaving at any time." Nate was studying the screen. "If she walked by we should have seen her."

Chris's arms were crossed tightly, covering his chest. He was swaying back and forth, from side-to-side, and was nervously chewing his lip again. His anxiety was mounting and his mind was racing. *They keep going over and over everything. How many times do I need to say the same thing?*

Nate went over what they were seeing, one more time, "There was no movement after Nickole dropped her off. The camera didn't pick up anything, until Chris backed the truck into his driveway."

"My phone says that at 5:27 a.m. my garage door was left open," Chris stated. "It says it was shut during the day. Maybe when Nickole was trying to get in the door around noon it broke the laser because my alarm was already going off." Chris's justification was wobbly as he weaved in and out of his thought process.

"I know Nickole tried the front door, but she couldn't get in because of the internal locks," Officer Coonrod responded.

"Yeah, those locks are there so the kids can't get out. Our remote, on the outside, doesn't work anymore. It got wet," Chris explained.

Officer Coonrod addressed Nate, "Alright, appreciate your time."

Chris quickly reached over to shake Nate's hand.

"Hopefully something comes up dude," Nate offered.

Chris turned briskly and sprinted to the front door. When he reached it, he turned and looked back at the officer.

"Do you just want to go talk to the detective? I want to get Nate's info real quick." Office Coonrod released Chris, who gladly left the house.

Nate looked at Officer Coonrod, "He's not acting right!"

"No?"

"He's rocking back and forth. He never loads his truck out of the garage, ever!"

Nate and Officer Coonrod looked at the video one more time, trying to make sense of the situation. Nate pointed to the screen, "See, Chris gets out and walks back and forth a couple of times. When he loads his truck he normally just walks over to it. He never backs it up. He told me someone had been trying to get into his tool box, so I suggested he park the truck in front of my house. I told him my camera would catch them if they tried again. He usually just brings a lunch box, a computer bag, and a water jug."

Officer Coonrod listened, evaluating the situation.

Nate continued, "And, the fact that he is explaining things, over and over. He doesn't look worried. He looks like he is trying to cover his tracks. If he is loading the back of his truck why is he walking back and forth on the passenger's side? The other weird thing that caught our attention, was where he parked when Shanann was out of town. He put his truck across the street in front of my house and parked her car all the way down the street. He is acting really suspicious," Nate offered his explanation to Nickole who had come back in the room. "He is normally so subdued. He told the officer three times what he put in his truck. He never talks. The fact that he is rambling on and on, makes me suspicious."

Officer Coonord replied, "Yeah, but put yourself in his shoes. He doesn't know what to do."

"Yeah, I know, but why he is so concerned that you know what he was putting in his truck instead of talking about the fact that we didn't see anyone? That's all I'm saying."

Officer Coonrod left the house and rejoined Chris on his front lawn.

Two officers approached Chris in the front of his house. The detective asked Chris about the doorbell camera and they came to the determination that no one was on the porch from the time Shanann came home around 2:00 a.m. until Nickole came to the front door looking for her around noon.

"The weird thing is, the garage door indicator said it was left open, after I left for work this morning. It might have been a sensor thing, but my phone doesn't show that it was shut. Nickole said it was shut when she came to the house around noon," Chris repeated his story as they all entered the house.

Officer Coonrod showed the detective Shanann's purse. It was sitting on the counter; wallet, medicine, phone, work planner, everything she religiously carried had been abandoned in the kitchen.

"The kids need medication as well, and their medicine is still here," Officer Coonrod pointed out.

The detective looked closely though the entire home. He got down on his hands and knees and directed his flashlight. He inspected the moldings, the carpet on the stairs, the walls, and the closets. *Nothing obvious.*

"The bed is stripped. Chris said she was in bed sleeping when he left. I looked and didn't see anything," Officer Coonrod stated.

The detective looked through the pillows and everything near the bed. A small point of light from the detective's flashlight located a picture of Chris and Shanann. It was a picture of the two of them, a loving couple in the center of the frame. Messages, and sweet notes of love and luck were handwritten on the matting around the picture.

"The only thing missing are the kid's blankets, like, their 'binkies'. Chris said they won't go anywhere without them," Officer Coonrod reported.

"And they're gone?"

"Yep. Car seats are in the car. Keys are in the center console of the car. Her cash, all of her ID, everything is still here. Phone is here," Officer Coonrod explained.

They continued to search the bathrooms and the kid's rooms.

"She's a stay-at-home mom and she does all of her work from home. She does it all on her phone. Her phone was on the upstairs couch, turned off."

The officers went out on the back porch to have a look around the yard, as Officer Coonrod explained how he couldn't get in the front door or the back door, because of the internal locks. "Chris said the garage door opener didn't work. I think he hid his garage door opener when he got here. Anyone who left the house had to leave through the garage."

The officers and detectives completed their search as well as they could. They would need to do a more complete search if Shanann didn't turn up. As they wrapped up and turned to leave the house Officer

Coonrod spoke to Chris. "We'll be in touch Chris. If you hear anything let us know."

The detectives drove away and Chris entered his eerily quiet house. He was relieved to be alone, away from the police, away from the questions and away from the video. The detectives had gone through his entire house for what seemed like hours. Every inch of his home had been searched, rummaged through, and essentially invaded. He knew the police were just doing their job, but, so much for privacy. He really needed to wash the girl's sheets. It was imperative they be washed. They smelled, and he couldn't get that smell out of his nose. He used extra detergent when he put them in the washing machine. Chris went down stairs and didn't take him long to realize the living room carpet had been stepped all over. Chris turned on ESPN, pulled out the vacuum cleaner, and proceeded to vacuum the entire downstairs. After rolling up the cord and tucking the machine back into its proper location, Chris made himself a power-shake. Chris's phone went off, indicating that he had a text. It was the realtor he had reached out to earlier in the day. He read the text on his phone:

Anne: There's a house in your neighborhood, looks like the same model.

Confirming 3 car garage.

Chris: Yes, a 3-car garage. I will drive by the address and check it out.

Anne: Is Shanann ok? She hasn't weighed in all day.

Chris: She hasn't been around all day. It's very odd.

Anne: That's weird, you must be worried? Have you checked with her friends or   called   and reported her missing?

Chris: I've done it all. Police are handling it now. Send prayers please.

Anne: Omg – I'm so sorry. Lots of prayers.

Chris put his phone on the couch as he sat silently. ESPN was on, but it was hard to concentrate, and that smell! Chris answered numerous phone calls and text messages. He was exhausted but he knew sleep was not coming any time soon and he spent much of the night on his phone. The entire situation was a nightmare.

***

Nate watched the video of Chris in the driveway numerous times. He was in constant phone communication with Sandy and Frank, Shanann's parents, who were in North Carolina. Nate could hear the agony and the frustration in their voices. They must be going through hell. He couldn't imagine not knowing where his wife and child were. He watched the tape one more time, maybe he was missing something. *It is so weird that Chris backed into the driveway. He never loaded his truck like that.* Nate stared at the TV again, the same thing. *Chris walked to the side of the truck three times and put something in the back seat. He put a gas can in the back of his work truck. There has got to be something else here. Maybe someone slipped into the garage when Chris left for work and was in the house with Shanann and the girls. Chris said he had issues with the garage door indicator. Maybe someone took them out, without being detected.* Nate instinctively knew that wasn't probable, but he didn't want to believe Chris could hurt his family. He saw Chris regularly, and while they weren't close, he seemed like a regular guy. Chris was constantly outside with his girls; taking them for walks in their wagon, mowing the lawn while they were swinging, watching them ride their bikes. He saw Chris much more often than Shanann. Nate knew from Sandy, that Shanann worked her tail off and had a very busy life. Sandy, Frank, Chris, and Shanann were all living next door when Nate and his family moved in. The neighborhood was quiet and while the houses were enormous inside, the back yard was a stone-throw away. Nate and Sandy quickly engaged in conversation, while standing on their back porches. As extraverts, they shared in neighborhood, small talk almost immediately. They discussed the kids, the dogs, the yard, the grills, and the weather.

Nate was having a difficult time wrapping his mind around this whole ordeal. It had been un-nerving seeing Chris not acting like a guy who was searching for his wife and little girls. None of this made sense. The only way Shanann and the girls could have left the house, was in Chris's truck. A chill ran down Nate's spine. Ignoring his instincts, he played out every possible scenario in his mind trying to think of a way someone could have entered the house, and taken Shanann and the girls. His desire to believe Chris's story was strong, but people don't just vanish into thin air. He wanted desperately to find a clue, something on that blasted video, anything that might offer an explanation. The alternative was too gruesome to comprehend. *Chris was in my house. He shook my hand and he is sleeping next door. Had Chris done something unthinkable to his family?* Nate shuddered at the possibility. He thought of his own small son, and went into hyper protective mode. Nate could still hear what Officer Coonrod had said, on his way out of the house, "I suggest you don't say anything to Chris that might set him off." The statement added to the gravity of the situation and possibilities flooded Nate's mind. What if there was a predator in the neighborhood? *Okay, I have to stick to the facts. Shanann and the girls are gone. Something horrible may have happened and no one has enough information to know anything for certain.*

That night before bed, Nate took the pistol out of his gun safe. He loaded it and put it under the bed. It was difficult to drift off and each time he did something would suddenly awaken him. Several times he went into the bedroom where his six-year-old son was sleeping. He knew his child was safe, his dogs were the best security system he had. He couldn't pinpoint the fear he was feeling, but it was real and it kept prompting him to check on his son. His little dude was sleeping soundly. When he turned to leave his child's bedroom, his wife was standing by the door. She had been checking in on their boy as well. They looked at one another and shared the same thought. *I hope Shanann and those girls are safe.*

Chapter 3

The phone startled Chris when it rang. He looked at the time, 9:00 a.m.

"Hello," Chris answered the phone sleepily.

"Hey Chris, this is Nickole. Have you heard anything yet?"

"No, it's been a really rough night." Chris looked at the clock. "I've only been asleep for two hours."

"Have you spoken to the press?"

"My phone rang like crazy last night, but I didn't answer if I didn't recognize the number."

"I think maybe you need to talk to the press. Maybe someone knows something. Maybe somebody has seen Shanann," Nickole's voice drifted off in worry.

"Sandy told me not to talk to them," Chris explained.

"I know, she told me too, but we have to do everything we can to find them," Nickole's voice broke, and he could tell she had been crying. "Chris, the press reached out to me. A news team will be at your house at 10:30," Nickole declared. "Please talk to them."

Chris put down his cell phone. *Okay this is probably the only way they will leave me alone.* Chris went upstairs to shower. He put on a new black and white printed sport shirt, a pair of shorts, trimmed his mustache and brushed his teeth. When the TV crew showed up at his door they were polite and eager to get his statement. Chris jumped right in and they began taping him on the front porch. He was nervous at first, but the crew made him feel comfortable and he stepped right into the interview regarding his missing wife and daughters.

"The most important thing is, like, wherever they are at, like, I have no inclination where they are at right now. I have thought of every friend I know of. All my friends, even called friends that might even know Shanann. It's like she just vanished. When I got home yesterday, it was like a ghost town. She wasn't here. The kids weren't here. I have no idea where they went. It's just earth shattering. I don't feel like this is even real. It's like a nightmare and I just can't wake up," Chris was even mannered. His tone steady.

"Chris, when did you learn that they weren't here?" the reporter inquired.

"I texted her a few times, called her, and didn't get a response. That was a little off. Then her friend, Nickole, showed up a little after noon, and I saw her on the doorbell camera. I asked her what was going on, and she said she couldn't get hold of Shanann. And I was, like, okay something's not right if she's not answering the door, and Nickole said her car was here. I knew I needed to get home, and when I got here and went inside no one was here, nothing," Chris continued to be measured in his answers. While the words were expressing concern, his facial expressions, and eyes, seemed void of emotion.

"So, I read that Shanann was going to take the girls to school, or something."

"Yeah, Bella was going to start kindergarten next Monday and they were just getting ready to start back again."

"Your friend Nickole tipped you off that something was wrong?"

"Yeah, Nickole was here at the front door, and if Shanann wasn't answering anybody else, this is not like her. Shanann works for a direct sales business and

41

answering the phone is what she does. For her not to respond to any of her people is weird. I mean if she doesn't respond to me that's fine, she's busy and she's got something going on, but not to respond to any of her people, that was not like her." Chris's arms were crossed tightly, as if he were hugging his chest, and he was gently rocking from side to side.

"What went through your mind when you didn't know what was going on?"

"I was trying to get home as fast as I could. I was blowing through stop lights just trying to get home as fast I could, because none of this made sense. I mean, if she wasn't here, where did she go? Who can I call? Who do I know that she could be with? If she went to a friend's house, where could she be staying? We went through everybody, everyone in my contact list and everyone in Nickole's contact list. Nothing has come up. Everyone said they haven't heard from her either. I am just hoping, right now, that she's somewhere safe. Maybe she is, but right now if she's vanished, I want her back so bad. I want those kids back so bad," Chris went on. He offered a pleasant smile when he spoke about Shanann and the girls coming back, and then returned to the interview. His face remained neutral, his voice was steady and unemotional.

"So, you mentioned that your first thought was where they might be, and then your second thought was that you were afraid people might think you have done something to them."

"Everyone is going to have their own opinion on this, but I just want everyone to know that I want my family back. I want them safe and I want them here. This house is not the same. Last night I was tripping. I can't stay in this house again, with no one here. Last night I wanted that knock on the door. I wanted the kids to run in and barrel rush me and knock me on the ground, but that didn't happen," Chris's appeal was not frantic. It was almost scripted as if he was playing a part of a concerned parent and husband.

"Who are you going to stay with tonight?"

"Probably my friends Nick and Amanda, unless something develops in the next few hours, or so. I'm hoping that someone has seen something, or knows something and comes forward," Chris continued, looking deliberate, slightly chewing on his lip.

"What's the hardest part of all this?"

"Not knowing. I don't know if they are safe, or if they're in trouble. There is that variable. I can't do anything right now, where I'm at. Are they safe huddled up somewhere, or are they in trouble? Knowing they could be in trouble, is earth shattering and it doesn't feel real," Chris continued. His words implied an anguish that was not revealed in his face or his voice.

"It sounds like everything was locked up and there was no sign of them leaving the house."

Chris agreed, "We have the doorbell camera and the neighbor has a camera. Everything's checked out."

"Were all the doors around the house locked?"

"The front door was locked. The garage door was unlocked, and that's normal, but the back sliding-door was locked."

"How could she leave if all of the doors are locked?"

"I don't want to put anything out there, but I suspect that someone pulled in the back where they can drive in. We have new townhomes back there." Chris slightly shrugged his shoulders and continued, "It's so hard to tell. We don't have cameras in the back yard or anything. It's hard to even suspect anything now as to how she could have left, if someone came and picked her up, or if someone took her." Chris listed the three possibilities, all projected in a matter-of-fact, monotone voice. "The reality is that there are cops everywhere, and K-9 units. I have never seen anything like this in my lifetime unless it was on TV or a movie. This doesn't seem real at all. It just seems like I am living in a nightmare that I can't get out of. I just want them home so bad," Chris's plea for his family was subdued, as if he were in shock or maybe ordering a pizza.

"You had the kids when Shanann was out of town. Did you see your wife when she got home?"

Chris answered, as his look went from totally passive to stern. "Yeah, I had the kids over the weekend. She got home late, about 2:00 a.m. She got back from Arizona. I saw her when she got home, but it was really quick, because it was 2:00 a.m. I saw the kids in the monitor before I left and that was it," Chris wasn't amused, and he was finally showing emotion, not a concern or fear, but annoyance.

"What kind of efforts are going on to find them?"

"The Frederick Police Department has been on point. Officers, detectives, sergeants, and the K-9 units are getting scents. Hopefully they can pick up something and maybe lead us to where they are right now," Chris's emotional moment had passed.

"Where did you get that shirt?"

"Shanann picked it up online, this is my favorite sports team in North Carolina."

"Wasn't she just there?"

"Yeah, she could have picked it up when she was there instead of Amazon. I like these shirts a lot," Chris responded to the small talk with a smile. His arms relaxed a bit and one hand went into his shorts pocket. He seemed to appreciate the momentary reprieve from the difficult questions.

"Describe your girls to us."

Chris tightened up again. His arms immediately crossed firmly against his chest and he started rocking from side to side. "Celeste, she's just a ball of energy. We call her rampage. She has two speeds, go and sleep. She's the trouble maker, always jumping off things and yelling at you. Bella is the calm, cautious, mothering type. She's more like me. She's calm. Celeste has her mom's personality. She is always gung-ho," Chris smiled as he spoke about his daughters.

"What do you want to say to the viewers?"

"I just want my family back."

"Okay, thanks Chris." The reporter wished Chris good luck and began wrapping up the segment.

Chris was more than relieved to step away from the camera. He was anxious to return to the organized, structured, safety inside the walls of his home. Chris entered the house and immediately closed and locked the front door. He wanted to lock out the chaos, the police stopping every car in the neighborhood, the detectives going door-to-door, the drones, the K-9 dogs, the reporters and the questions, too many questions! He needed a way to steady himself. He took a deep breath and slipped back into his program, his routine. He needed normal. His phone rang and he took the call.

In North Carolina, Sandy, Frank, and Shanann's brother Frankie were frantic with worry and fear. *Where are they? What happened?* Sandy asked the questions over and over. She called Nate and Nickole when the panic became too much to bear, when the anxiety of not hearing anything consumed all of her energy, and threatened her composure. Shanann's parents, and brother were not witnessing the activity of the police, the drones, the K-9 search, and the worried neighbors. They felt like they were a million miles away and could do absolutely nothing!

Sandy thought about the time she had spent with her daughter and grandchildren in Colorado. Shanann had been diagnosed with lupus and some days her pain was all-consuming. She had been told that she would not be able to have children, but she beat the odds. Bella Marie was born on December 17, 2013, and they all thanked God every day for their little miracle baby. Shanann's devotion to her first daughter was limitless, and when she became pregnant with her second child, she felt doubly blessed. Unfortunately, her health became a serious concern when her lupus flared up. Sandy and Frank sold everything, but their house, in North Carolina, and moved to Colorado to help Shanann get through her second pregnancy. Shanann didn't go out much during her pregnancy. She was weak and experienced an onslaught of symptoms. Sandy hated watching Shanann when she was ill and suffering from a debilitating illness. Living together was not always the easiest process, but they managed, and when Celeste Cathryn was born on July 17, 2015, the entire family was ecstatic. Sandy had been there for fifteen months when she decided it was time to go back to North Carolina. She missed her house and wanted to go home. She had completed what she had set out to do. Adorable baby CeCe had arrived, and Shanann was on her feet.

Where are my girls? The fear of the unknown was threatened only by the fear of hearing the unthinkable. Shanann and the children had just spent six weeks with Sandy, Frank, and Frankie. They played on the beach, laughed in the rain, and gleefully stomped through puddles. They hugged the girl's sweet faces, helped them brush their teeth, and read them bedtime stories. They celebrated CeCe's third birthday. The idea that something had happened to them was too much to consider. They had to be safe. They just had to be. Something was terribly wrong, but what? They knew that things between Shanann and Chris were not perfect, that something seemed to be bothering him, but trial was part of marriage. Chris and Shanann had faced so much, and Chris had never been anything but supportive to Shanann. Sandy loved that Chris had been so caring and attentive to her daughter. Chris had once let Shanann sleep in his lap for almost three hours, when she was having a grueling day. He never said a word, never attempted to move Shanann as she slept peacefully. He just sat there, dutifully holding her head in his lap, even though he really had to pee. Chris had always been the most adoring husband to Shanann and an amazing father to the girls. However, Chris did seem a bit off when he joined his family in North Carolina, for the final week of their vacation. He had snapped at the girls, and when Sandy was following him in the car she had to drive well over the speed limit just to keep up with him, which was very unusual. The night he arrived, Shanann became violently ill and couldn't keep anything down. Frankie had stepped in, checking on his sister, making certain she was okay. Chris seemed indifferent to the fact that his pregnant wife was ill as he slept in another room. After a week, Chris and Shanann took the girls home to Colorado, even though Sandy asked her daughter to stay.

While Sandy and Frank tried to think positive thoughts, the logical intervened. Shanann would have never left the house without her phone, her wallet, and the girl's medicine. Shanann was organized, structured and always had a plan. She would never leave in a spontaneous moment or in a rush and not take those items. *Oh my God, where is my daughter?* Sandy called Nate again.

"Hi Nate, anything new? Have you heard anything?"

"Hi Sandy. Chris did an interview for one the stations and it should be on the news later this evening."

"What is he thinking? He was the last one to see her. What if he compromises an investigation?"

"I'm not sure. Hey, I've got to go, someone is at the front door. I will call if anything comes up."

"Okay thanks!"

Nate held back his barking dogs as he opened the door.

"Hi, I'm with CNN news. We were hoping to get a statement regarding the Watts' family."

"No comment, sorry!" Nate shut the door and tried to shut out the chaos that was occurring all around his home. *This is crazy!*

Sandy, Frank and Frankie waited impatiently for the national news. "Look Frank, it is the headline story," Sandy exclaimed, fear in her voice.

"Pregnant Shanann Watts, and her two young daughters are still missing tonight in Frederick, Colorado, as Chris Watts pleads for the return of his family." The news anchor launched into the story.

Frank, Sandy, and Frankie silently watched Chris speak about Shanann and the girls. They anxiously saw him plead for his family without emotion, without sadness, without commitment. Chris finished speaking and a commercial began. Frank turned off the TV. The horror in the room was palpable

"Oh my God, Frank, Chris did something to them," Sandy spoke the words as if they were poison pouring off her tongue.

Frank was livid. *This is not my son-in-law. Who is this person and what has he done with my family?*

"Frank, he doesn't even seem concerned," Sandy said, mystified. "Do you think, oh my God?" Sandy began to cry and curse at the same time.

Frank immediately called the Frederick Police Department and asked to speak to the detective who was over-seeing the investigation.

"If you want to find my daughter access the GPS on Chris's truck. Then you'll find my family." Frank hung up the phone, a shiver of terror shot though his body.

Chapter 4

The room was dark and cold. Shanann was having a hard time remembering. Thoughts seemed to dip into her awareness and then fade out just as quickly. There was something, a heavy thought that evaded her. Something crept close to the edges of her mind and then quickly dodged her intention like a thief in the night. The more she tried to retrieve the memory the foggier everything became. The memory was unbearably heavy, yet the path was empty; no clues, no recognition, no clarity. She sat silently in the looming darkness of her living room. Joy seemed far away and unreachable. She tried to remember the light in the kitchen, the smell of flowers, the feel of Nico's skin and CeCe's smile, but they were all fading. Shanann looked around the room. The creeping darkness seemed to be a living entity, above her and below her, consuming her. Shanann forced herself to pay attention. As she grasped for awareness, she realized that everything in her living room was gone. The pictures on the walls, the sofa, the rugs. All of it was gone. *What is happening to me? Why I am I alone?* Shanann smelled the sage before she heard the drum. *He's here.* She remembered the long braid, the deep brown eyes, the gentle voice, and the connection she had felt with him. *Speaks With Stars, yes that's his name.* Shanann walked quickly to the front door and looked out. *Yes, it's him.* A feeling of relief washed over her as she rushed outside.

"You're here," she said quietly.

"You are not alone," he replied gently, as he stoked the small fire in the middle of the yard.

"All of my things, everything in my house, everything is gone."

"How do you feel, right now?"

Shanann thought it was a strange question. She pondered for a moment. *How do I feel right now?* Once she thought about it the answer seemed clear. "Empty! I feel empty!"

"And your home is, empty?"

Shanann had a moment of recognition, "My thoughts emptied my home?"

"Your thoughts and your feelings emptied your home," he stated.

Shanann looked confused.

"The laws of nature are much different here."

Shanann let the idea dwell in her mind for a moment. This was all so strange.

"How old do you think I am?" he asked.

Shanann shrugged her shoulders, "Thirty-five, maybe?"

"I died when I was sixty-five-years old. I choose to look like this. I prefer being young and strong. Your son, what did he look like when you saw him?"

"He was a newborn," Shanann answered thoughtfully.

"He wanted you to see him that way. He knew it would be easier for you to see him in the timeline you are used to."

"You mean, Nico could have been Bella's age?"

"Of course, but your mind would have rejected the idea. You are used to seeing your children as they grow, in the stages of the physical body. They are not as attached to their physical images. They lived in them a much shorter time than we did."

Shanann sat down on the porch. This was so confusing. She tried to wrap her mind around the concept. *My son is protecting me by appearing as a newborn, and my dark mood made my furniture disappear.* "Wait, if there is so much freedom to navigate here, why can't I just think of Bella and she will appear?"

"Bella has her own free will. She is not restricted by the needs of a four-year-old, like she was before. Perhaps she has something of importance that she must do."

"What could she need more than being with me?"

"Only she can answer that question."

Shanann sat on her front porch steps. She looked at the interesting stranger, now friend, who sat by his fire in her front yard. Shanann thought of the emptiness in her house and the emptiness in her heart. *If my furniture can disappear because of my mood, will I disappear into this deep depression I am sinking into?* The thought was over-whelming and Shanann felt a tear roll down her cheek.

Speaks With Stars was moved by her sadness, "You will never disappear, but souls can become lost in their own darkness. I have seen some of my people so consumed with grief they can no longer find their way. When I see them, I remind them they are not alone. They can let go of their pain if they chose to do so. There are some who have trouble letting go."

"How do you let go?"

"You must confront the darkness that is looming in your heart and mind."

"Then there is hope?" Shanann tearfully asked.

Speaks With Stars smiled slightly, "There is always hope. The soul is and always will be full of joy and abundance. The mind shuts out the soul. It clings to fear and suffering in an attempt to reconcile it, to make sense of it. It is up to the heart to bring the two together," Speaks With Stars looked deeply into her eyes. "You must face what you fear by embracing what you love!"

Shanann nodded in appreciation and went into her home. A memory filled her entire being when she walked through the front door. Bella had been standing in the living room, looking outside. It was raining and hailing. There were thunderous noises and Bella had been so frightened. Shanann brought her downstairs to show her that the storm was not going to hurt her.

"Mommy our street is going to get broken," Bella had said with great concern.

Shanann told her that everything was fine, that the rain would not harm her or the street, and she assured Bella that they were safe in their own home. Shanann could see her little princess looking out the front door, covering her ears. It seemed like more than a memory. She remembered thinking of how often it rained in North Carolina. She had been excited to take the girls to visit family for six weeks. She remembered hearing CeCe upstairs, covering her tiny ears to keep the thunder out of her bedroom. She was in her little nightie holding her 'binkie' tightly while Chris comforted her. Shanann had peaked in CeCe's bedroom and remembered thinking how much she appreciated Chris. He was stretched out on CeCe's bed trying to block out her fear of the storm. As he read CeCe's favorite story, Shanann had felt a deep contentment. After so many hard years of pain and burden, she was finally in a really great place. They had financial worries, but who didn't? They would figure that out. After everything she had gone through, they were on the right track. She loved her husband, adored her girls, and was feeling strong and healthy. And she knew Chris truly loved her. He showed her in so many ways. He did the laundry and the shopping. He bathed the girls and read them stories, and he was so supportive of her business. She knew he didn't enjoy being part of her FaceTime, taping the videos, but he did it without complaining. He did it for her job, for their family, He was always affectionate, holding her hand or giving her a sweet kiss. Shanann remembered the birthday message she posted on social media in May, not that long ago, in a time she was familiar with.

"Today I celebrate you! Chris, you are absolutely the BEST thing that ever happened to me. In 2010 you were placed in my life. I was at my worst! I was just diagnosed with Lupus and Fibro and I felt like my world was crumbling around me! Then I met you! We have so many incredible memories from these past 8 years. We have two beautiful girls, sold our house, moved halfway across the world, built a home for our family, and you constantly do for us! You work your ass off, you're an amazing husband and an even better dad! You are the blessing I've been looking for my whole life! You are chasing big goals, and dreams, and you never stop. You support me in so many ways! I hope you have an amazing Birthday! I love you baby!"

Shanann saw a bolt of lightning through the window, followed by a deafening blast of thunder that jolted her from the memories, back to her current situation. The feelings of wonder and blessing were suddenly swept away by a blast of cold air that blew the front door wide open. Rain and hail poured into the living room as she tried to get the front door closed. It was heavy and difficult to move. She was soaking wet and shivering from the frigid, whirling wind. After much effort, she finally managed to close the door. Standing in the darkness of her living room, the walls seemed to swell up as if they were sucking the goodness of life from her. The dark feeling that was stuck in her soul, like a festering sliver, suddenly burst into her awareness. A thought that had been circling the edges of her mind, a thought that was threatening darkness and total loss. She knew what it was, betrayal. Memories came rushing in, but they were fragmented. A restaurant receipt for two, denial, another woman. Bits and pieces, like broken glass, cut into her love for him, cut into their marriage, cut through their commitment, severed their family. Shanann remembered picking up Chris at the airport in North Carolina. When she had left, only five weeks prior, he couldn't keep his hands off of her. When he arrived in North Carolina, everything was different.

Chris had spoken words she could never imagine, "I'm scared to death about this third baby. I'm happy with just Bella and CeCe. We aren't compatible anymore."

Feelings of complete desperation engulfed her as the memories flooded in. *How do I make him feel more compatible if he isn't giving me anything? Chris has changed, I don't know him anymore. He hasn't touched me, or kissed me, or even talked to me. What if he really doesn't love me anymore? How can I do this alone with three kids?* Shanann remembered crying alone in the bedroom of her parent's home in North Carolina, crying until sleep offered a moment of silence, a temporary reprieve.

Shanann's agonizing memories were suddenly interrupted when she heard a noise outside on the porch. *Bella?* She ran to the door and pushed it open, against the force of the howling wind and torrents of rain.

A small figure was huddled against the house, apparently trying to avoid being blown away by the tremendous storm. Shanann could see immediately that it was not her Bella. She made her way over to the shivering body and could see that it was a young woman. She touched her on the shoulder and the woman turned. Shanann could see a deep sadness in her eyes.

"Come inside, out of the storm." She didn't know if the woman could hear her over the sound of thunder and the howling wind. The woman got up, hiding her face from the pouring rain, and followed Shanann into the house.

"I am going to try and find some blankets to warm you up," Shanann told the shivering woman. Much to Shanann's surprise her home was not empty. The furniture, the pictures, the girl's toys, everything was just where it had been. Shanann ran up the stairs and pulled a blanket and two towels out of the linen closet. When she came down, she found the woman sitting in a corner in the living room. She was sitting low to the floor, yet still on her feet, like she was ready to pounce. Shanann could see that the young woman was Native American, probably in her early thirties. Her hair was long, coal black, and soaking wet. The woman turned her head and Shanann saw a sadness in her brown eyes that made her shudder. Shanann slowly walked over to her and handed her a towel.

"It's for your hair." Shanann pointed to her own hair. The woman tentatively took the towel and started to dry with it. She was still shivering when Shanann took the blanket and gently wrapped it around her shoulders. The woman seemed to be comforted by the blanket and the generosity. She spoke softly in what seemed to be her native language, but Shanann had no idea what she was saying. The woman motioned toward the door as if there was something outside that was important to her.

"I'm sorry, I don't understand you. Why don't you try to rest now?" Shanann suddenly felt very tired. She went to her recently retrieved sofa and laid down. She didn't intend to fall asleep, with the woman sitting in the corner of her living room, but she did.

When Shanann woke up, the woman was not there. The towels and blankets were neatly folded on the table. A small bracelet lay on top of them. *A thank you gift?* She picked up the bracelet and put it on her wrist. Shanann went outside hoping that Speaks With Stars was near. She wanted to see if he knew who the young woman was. She went out on the porch and thought of him. She smelled the sage and saw him near a small fire. She walked over to him and sat on a hollow log close to the fire. The sky was clear, and a giant rainbow folded over them.

"There was a woman on my porch during the storm. She seemed lost," Shanann reported. "I brought her in and put a blanket around her so she could warm up. Do you know her?"

"Where did you find a blanket? I thought your possessions were all gone."

"That is the strange part, I heard her crying in the storm, and when I brought her in the house, all my things were back, everything right in its place. I fell asleep, and when I woke up she was gone. She left me this little bracelet."

"Did she speak to you?"

"Yes, she was saying something, but I couldn't understand her."

"Her name is Silver Moon. She lived on the Sand Creek many years ago. Her people were all killed. She watched, one by one, as they were slaughtered by the English-speaking soldiers. She knows your language, but she will never speak it out of respect for those who died."

"Was she the only one who survived?"

"No, she was the last one murdered."

Shanann felt a cold shiver go down her spine. "How long has she been wandering?"

"Her spirit left her human body, one hundred and fifty-four years ago, but in a place with no time, who can say?" Speaks With Stars saw the confusion on Shanann's face. He smiled with understanding. "People are taught to measure almost everything with time. When I was young, we judged the days by the sky and the seasons. We knew when to hunt and gather so we did not starve during the long winters. I knew when I was expected to go through my ritual, when I would leave boyhood and become a man."

Shanann pondered the idea for a few moments, and then began reflecting on her own experience.

"Wow, I can't think of anything in my life that is not directed from time. Time to get the girls up, time for their medicine, FaceTime, time for school, time for meals. I even set a time to be worried about the bills. Always a playdate or a phone call or a text." Shanann sat in silence once again, thinking about her life. "When I was sick, I spent a lot of time in pain, unable to do anything. I think I wanted to make up for lost time by fitting everything I could into each day."

"In this place, there is no such thing as lost time. There is only now."

Shanann sat by the crackling fire, in the silence. She touched the bracelet that she was wearing. "Silver Moon seemed very sad. Did she have children and a husband?"

"Silver Moon had a husband she loved very much, and she had two children who were very young. She also had a big belly. Her child was trying to be born the day the soldiers came. She hid on the side of their camp in a big, hollow tree. She watched as they killed everyone she loved, including her young children. She took a piece of her pouch and bit on it while her child made his way into the world. She never made a sound, but when the newborn filled his lungs with air, he let out a cry and the soldiers found them. They took her new baby and tossed him in the dirt to die. They did not care that she had just given birth, and they took her for their own pleasure before they killed her."

Shanann was overcome with Silver Moon's story. "My God, no wonder she was crying."

"Silver Moon's tears were not for her own loss. She was crying for you. She was drawn to you and your anguish. She understands it, and she wanted to comfort you. She wanted to share your grief and let you know that she is with you. You were kind to her, not knowing her story. She was grateful that in your own grief, you found compassion for a stranger. Your kindness filled your heart, and…"

Shanann interrupted him, "And filled my house."

Speak with Stars smiled.

"Will I ever see her again?"

"I am not sure, but she will always be with you."

"Will Silver Moon go to the light?" Shanann asked.

"When people are so filled with love, they are the light." Speaks With Stars, smiled and took a long draw from his pipe.

Shanann looked intently at her new friend, and then slowly walked to the front door of her home. As if pondering the world, Shanann made her way up the long staircase and went directly to Bella's bedroom. Such great care had gone into decorating this room for her firstborn. The lavender walls, the ottoman and glider Gran had given her, the large black and white prints of mommy and daddy hanging on the walls; all were designed to give Bella a sense of belonging in her own very special place. *Bella Marie* was spelled out in a lovely cursive font, adding to the uniqueness of the spacious room. Butterflies danced about her bed while she slept peacefully and dreamt four-year-old dreams. Shanann went to the closet and pulled out one of Bella's favorite dresses, one with little spaghetti straps. She pulled it close to her and smelled it, hoping for a hint of her daughter. Shanann sat down on the bed, slightly leaning against the black tufted headboard. She picked up Bella's white stuffed kitty and held it closely. Gran and Speaks With Stars had assured her that Bella was okay, that she was not alone, but Shanann needed to see her, to hold her. She didn't understand why her little girl was not with her. Tears welled up in her eyes as she thought of everything that was happening. Chris had betrayed her. She confronted him about having an affair; they were fighting, crying, and she couldn't breathe, and then she was here. She missed her children, she missed her husband, and she missed her life. She wanted to talk to her mom and dad, and her Frankie. This was all so confusing. She thought of Silver Moon, and wondered how she had dealt with losing her family, all of her people. How had she coped with the sudden shock, the trauma of losing everything in a matter of minutes? She thought about Gran, so peaceful, so happy and content. Why wasn't she in that place yet? Bella! She needed to find her so they could escape this confusion and sorrow. She needed her daughter to leave with her, to go to the light, but how? Shanann lay down on the bed and snuggled deeply into Bella's comforter. She let the dancing butterflies take her to a place of comfort and she fell into a deep sleep.

***

Speaks With Stars went to his fire and strategically added kindling. He knew a lot of energy would be needed. He had ventured to the cliffs to pull from the great mother. Her energy was strong. Shanann had touched him deeply with her sensitivity and kindness, but mostly with her deep sadness, and her overwhelming need to find her daughter. He could feel Bella's presence, even though he did not know where she was. Some kind of extraordinary tragedy had happened to this woman and her children. Speaks With Stars wondered if those in the physical world knew what had happened yet, if the truth of their experience had been revealed. His fire needed to be high, his song strong, and the drumming powerful. Speaks With Stars inhaled deeply from his pipe. He began the mysterious dance, his song echoed loudly, and his drum kept the rhythm of his movements as he slipped into a trance. He saw Silver Moon in the shadows. This reaffirmed his suspicions. She only appeared when great tragedy had occurred. Her mercy and empathy seemed to be present when the horrific happened to the innocent. She had been a guide for many who did not understand what had happened to them. His path was to let the wandering souls know they were not alone. Not everyone was able to find the light they sought immediately. Some souls experienced unexpected trauma, and they needed to process their experiences before they could let go and move on. The people in the physical realm were even more difficult to reach. He would to go into a trance state and dance for clarity. His song and drumming were loud, and echoed through the great valley. The fire raged as he danced to the point of frenzy. Clues would be noticed for those in the physical world though his intention. Someone would hear his magic, and it might link them to a tragedy they did not yet fully understand.

***

–

The K9 search team went upstairs in the Watts' house. The officer and her excited lab partner, Cody, were joined by a police detective. They made their way methodically through the house looking for clues. The canine officer explained that Cody was trained to detect trauma. They headed to Shanann's office. Near a closet in the room, two square mirrors hung above a bulletin board that was leaning against the wall. It was covered with multicolored sticky notes, indicators of a very busy person. The canine officer took Cody and slowly entered the closet. It was painted a deep, dark pink and an entire wall held Shanann's shoes. There were purses, jackets, bags, and array of other accessories hanging on the opposite side of the closet. The small side of the closet was lined with inspirational notes and sayings.

"Well, there's plenty of her scent in here."

The officer responded with a resounding, "Yes."

Suddenly, there was a giggle. The canine officer was startled. "Oh my, what was that? What in the world was that? Go in there and step on that little blue thing and see if that's where that noise came from," she requested of her companion as she laughed nervously.

"Yeah, it sounded like a kid's toy," the other officer rationalized.

"It sort of sounded like it."

"Something! I heard it."

"Did you hear it?"

"I did," the officer declared as she made her way into the room looking for a toy or something that made the strange giggle sound.

The canine officer continued in a nervous voice, "It sounded like a kid giggling or something, didn't it?"

"It did," the officer replied.

She continued searching for a logical explanation for the sound as she retraced their steps.

"Where did that come from? Cody just walked in there. Well, that was strange. We'll make a note of that." The K9 officer was clearly surprised.

The other officer confirmed once again, "I heard it. I definitely heard the same thing you did."

"Yeah, and then Cody just sort of turned around and looked."

The two officers shook off their moment of astonishment and confusion and continued the search. Little dresses were hanging in the laundry room and the two officers went through them looking for a scent. Cody was excited to be doing his job. The officers continued to look methodically through the dresses and pajamas that belonged to Bella and Celeste. The scent of cleaner was strong. They left the laundry area and went into Bella's bedroom. The lavender walls and Bella's name above her bed declared ownership. The officer's highly trained canine partner barked loudly and was greatly excited. Cody stopped by Bella's bed and was very insistent that something of importance was nearby. He did not stop his excited bark until one of the officers looked under the bed. She pulled out Bella's book, "*All By Myself*," by Mercer Mayer. Cody immediately stopped barking.

"That's what he was showing you," the officer declared.

The threesome continued the deliberate search, snapping pictures, taking notes, and shining the flashlight into the darkest corners.

"It almost seems like this place is too immaculate to be normal."

"It's amazingly clean."

They continued into Celeste's bedroom. One of the officers commented that there was nothing under the bed.

"Yeah, Cody didn't react in here like he did before," she confirmed.

***

Speaks With Stars collapsed with exhaustion, his body leaning against the mighty rock. The wind was gentle, and cool. He pictured the room where he had first encountered Bella, a baby in her crib. He had been drawn to her spirit. He had felt the need to protect her, although he did not know why. He remembered how she looked directly at him. She had seen him as a physical man, as a friend, and she giggled with delight. They had established a deep, soulful connection, one that defied space and time. It was clear to him now why they had developed a strong bond.

Chapter 5

After Chris interviewed with the press, he was asked to come down to the office of the Colorado Bureau of Investigation. By 6:00 p.m. Chris was sitting in a small interrogation room. The rectangular table in the middle of the room offered limited sitting space. It was very cozy, or remarkably claustrophobic, depending on your point of view. Chris knew a K/9 team would be scouring his home in search for clues during this interview.

FBI agent, Graham Coder, entered the room. Chris was in the corner while Graham sat at the end of the table but on the same side. Chris faced him directly and was limited to a small area as Graham's position boxed him in. Agent Coder began the conversation, "Is there anything you want to start with?"

"I wonder if I caused this. Did I make her feel, like, she needed to leave? Did she really feel the things she was saying, like us falling out of love? Did that really register at the time, or did that come after I went to work? She was still there when I left. Did she lay there and just think, 'He doesn't love me. Should I just go?' She got home at 2:00 and I was passed out. My alarm went off at 4:00. I got dressed and brushed my teeth. We started talking about 4:15. I felt, like, I needed to speak with her, face to face. I got back in bed because I wanted to talk to her. She told me that she wanted to get up with me. I woke her up and started talking about being apart and figuring out who we are. The best way to see one another is when you are apart. The last week I went to North Carolina, when we were together, that spark wasn't there. The connection we had is not there anymore. The love is gone. If we want to stay together for the kids I don't think it is going to work." Chris paused and seemed deep in thought as though he needed to reaffirm, to himself, the things he was claiming.

He continued, "Having another baby isn't going to bring us back together. Separation is the best for us. When Shanann started crying it was hard, but we needed to do this face-to-face. She said she wanted things to work out. Most of the time when you have kids and fall out of love, lose your connection, bringing a new baby into the situation doesn't always work. It's almost better to separate. You don't want to be the couple parading around with a mask on for the kids. That's what I don't want. That's why we were talking about this. I was bawling my eyes out. We talked about selling the house. There is no way we can stay in this house and have another kid and keep everything afloat. We can move to Brighton or somewhere cheaper. Shanann had contacted a realtor the week before and I contacted Anne, the realtor, earlier that day. This was not like a big bang theory. It didn't come out of left field. We knew something was going to change. The conversations ended. I rolled out of bed and she said I'm taking the kids to a friend's house, but I'll be back later. I am 100% certain she said that. I wasn't sure why she wanted to leave. Hopefully, she went to see someone she can trust, and they have a kid so the girls can play with them."

FBI agent Coder nodded and prompted Chris, but let him speak freely.

"I texted her at 7:40 a.m. to see where she was taking the kids. Between 7:40 and noon I was working. Nickole tried to reach me at 1:00 p.m. She said Shanann was missing and she was going to call the cops. There were like fifty text messages when we found her phone, but her phone was turned off. It was at 50%. It was usually on the nightstand by the bed."

Chris paused and the only sound in the room was the large clock hanging on the wall, tick, tick, tick.

"I went into the bedrooms looking for everyone. I found the wedding ring on the night stand. She only takes it off when she colors her hair and she did that a week ago. I think she took it off because of the conversation we had. Nickole knew Shanann's pass code."

Agent Coder seemed a bit surprised that Shanann had given Nickole her pass code. He asked how long the women had known one another.

"Shanann and Nickole have known each other for about a year. Nickole worked with Sandy in Colorado and then she got into Le-Vel.

Chris continued, "At about 4:00 p.m. the police checked the neighbor's camera video. I signed paper work for them to search the house. I asked to stay outside. By 6:00 p.m. I was calling everyone."

Agent Coder asked Chris if he had been alone.

"I was by myself. At 7:30 p.m. Nick and Amanda came by to show their support. I am going to their house tonight. They may be waiting outside right now. I couldn't stay in my house again."

"And who are Nick and Amanda?" Agent Coder inquired.

"Amanda worked where the kids went to school and then she started with Le-Vel. Lauren was supposed to meet at our house for a pregnancy pal meeting."

"And who is Lauren?"

"She is a friend of Shanann's. They are both pregnant and get together to support one another," Chris continued, his answers scattered and a bit erratic.

"If she's at someone's house right now that would drive me crazy. She has got to be with someone that I don't know. Yesterday I would have said they walked out. Today I'm leaning the other direction. Friends were coming by to show their support. At 10:00 p.m. I was in bed answering the phone. Le-Vel friends and family were all calling." Chris named off a list of people.

"You had marital discord the day your wife went missing. What do you think about that?" Agent Coder asked.

"It makes me sick to my stomach. People are telling me this doesn't look good on me, if they know we were having trouble. This is something I would never do to my kids and wife, at all."

Chris started speaking again after formulating his thoughts, "I'm not sure how to make people believe that, but I would never harm anyone in my family!"

Chris emphatically repeated himself several times, "I promise our conversation had nothing to do with any of this."

"Are you telling me the truth? Why should I believe you?" Agent Coder finally tackled the elephant in the room.

"I am a very trust worthy person and the people who know me, know I'm calm. I'm not argumentative. I'm never going to be abusive or physical in any way. I would never harm my kids, I would never harm my wife. You can talk to any of my friends. They know me. I'm a low-key guy who is quiet. I avoid confrontation. If someone yells at me or screams at me I just take it. I just try to get things back to a cool conversation. I am not that person and I have never been that person," Chris insisted.

"Okay, I have a lot more questions for you. Questioning tonight is on a voluntary basis. Do you want to keep talking to me?" Agent Coder was very clear.

"I mean, I can, if you want, I can keep talking," Chris answered in compliance.

"You understand I'm not arresting you, and you understand you can walk out of here tonight?"

"Yes," Chris answered.

"Do you know where your wife is?" Agent Coder asked Chris directly.

"I don't know."

"Are you telling me the truth?"

"I'm telling you the absolute truth."

"Let's take a tiny break. Do you need to use the restroom? There is water or Gatorade if you need it. I'm going to step out for just a few minutes and look at my notes."

Chris was left alone with the only sound in the room, tick, tick, tick. He sighed deeply and tapped on the table a few times. Agent Coder reentered the room.

"How are you feeling?" He asked Chris.

"I'm looking at that picture." Chris looked down at picture of the girls that was lying on the table. "Celeste loved those shoes even though they are winter shoes."

"Those are her boots aren't they?" Agent Coder gave a little laugh, amused by the winter boots Celeste was wearing in a summer picture. *What a cutie.*

"Shanann was going to sell them on Facebook marketplace. They were sitting on the windowsill, when they got back from North Carolina. I guess CeCe saw them, and she proceeded to take them back. She has worn them every day since they got back. Even when it was one hundred degrees outside. She loved those boots. She always loved them," Chris spoke as if drifting in memory. He continued, "Bella, she always wore her flip flops. She loved that dress," Chris pointed out, referring to the pictures he was looking at. "She loved flip flops. CeCe loved that dress. She liked the buttons in the back," Chris's voice softened as he spoke of his daughters.

"Is CeCe short for something?" Agent Coder asked, drawing his attention back into the room.

"Celeste."

"Bella and Celeste. Tell me about them," Agent Coder prompted.

"Celeste, she's a rampage. She's a tiger. Bella, she's the calm mothering one. She's is always asking, "Are you okay? Are you fine?" She's just the sweetest little girl. She's the one who favors me the most and CeCe favors Shanann. When you see my baby pics Bella looks more like me."

"Is she daddy's girl?" Agent Coder asked.

"Celeste is. That is how it works, isn't it? With the first one I didn't really know what I was doing. The second one bonded with me right from the start."

"I remember CeCe wore that dress not too long ago." Chris paused as if he needed a moment of silence. He took a breath and continued, "That dress had little buttons in the back, and when she would get her pajamas on she would say, 'No daddy, buttons in the back'. Bella loved those spaghetti strap dresses. She likes long dresses. She was a girlie girl, always. I put CeCe in a Supergirl t-shirt and she loved it every time. CeCe was always smiling for the camera. Bella, you had to bribe with gum to get a smile. You're going to find them, right?"

"I need your help."

"I've got to find them and Shanann."

"Can you think of anything else you want to say now?"

"Just how much I want to see these two girls and my wife again. I want them home."

"I mentioned that when children go missing, with the FBI it's a lot like you see in the movies. We call every agent, wake them up, and get them out of bed. We even call them back from vacation. We like to put the full force in. Is that something you are comfortable with?"

"Yeah."

"That means that I want to have as many eyes, as many hands, as many investigative people as we can possibly get, looking at your house. Can we do that right this minute?"

"Yeah, I'll stay out of the way."

"That's usually best, for you, for us, for everyone."

"Can I stay at my friend's house then?" Chris asked with the hope of finally getting out of the room.

"Is that an option?" Agent Coder asked. "It will better if you're not at the house when they conduct the search."

"I'm not sure if my friends are still outside. I don't have my phone. I didn't have a signal in here anyway." Chris gave a little laugh, happy to be thinking about leaving.

"I might just slip out for a short break and say 'guys we should go in that house right now'. What is the code?"

Chris gave Agent Coder the code to the front door.

"That latch isn't going to get in our way?"

"It shouldn't. If it does just call me."

"And when we go in there I want them to run a black light over everything, looking for hair strands and

DNA samples. I want them to go over your stuff and your wife's stuff, everything. Do you have a problem with that?"

"That's fine," Chris said, seemingly unconcerned that his things would be on full view of an entire team.

"I am going to cut them lose to go over everything so we can find these girls." Agent Coder announced. "Can we keep talking about some complicated things that might make you uncomfortable? I think you know why I am going to ask difficult questions."

"It's a hard job," Chris offered.

"It is a hard job, and I'm going to ask you one thing and you're going to give me an answer, and I'm going to ask you the same thing in a slightly different way, and after about ten iterations of this you may get annoyed, but I have to make sure we understand each other, okay?"

"Yeah."

"So we have your daughters who are missing, and your wife who is missing and that is the most important thing right now. Do you agree with that? You have done a very good job speaking to me about the very hard conversation you guys had. That is sometimes hard, and I understand how someone might not want to tell me about a personal conversation. Like, 'please help find my kids and you don't need to know about my marriage argument'. So, you have done very well, and I need you to keep doing that. I need you to tell me about your marriage and infidelity."

"Okay, I have never cheated on my wife, and I fully suspect she has never done that to me. She's always been a trustworthy person. I've always been a trustworthy person. I fully suspect that if we ever thought about straying from one another, we would tell each other before it happened."

"I think that sounds ridiculous, because in the history of the earth nobody ever does that." Agent Coder laughed slightly.

Chris joined in, slightly laughing, "I mean that's how I like to think it would happen. I know people make mistakes, but in my head that's what I hope would happen."

"Now, even though I think that sounds ridiculous, if I were in your shoes I would say the exact same thing. And I believe that, but I kind of don't. In my job I meet all kinds of people, and there are guys who have Saturdays with their girlfriends and Sundays with their wives. They consider themselves to be very virtuous people. With that in mind I don't care if there has been anyone in your relationship. I'm not going to tell the press and I am not going to tell anyone, but I need to know. So is there anyone that you think your wife got close with?"

"If there was, it was very secretive because I had no inkling. There wasn't even a suspicion." Chris answered.

"Not one guy, or a girl?" Agent Coder prompted.

"If that was the case I didn't have one suspicion about it. If it happened, I wasn't aware. There was no texting, or hiding anything when I walked in the room."

"No perfume when she went out with the girls?"

"She always sprays something, but there wasn't anything special or odd."

"No late nights that surprised you?"

"No."

"On your end, I've got to ask, what's her name?

"I don't have another one," Chris answered nervously.

"Are you sure?"

"I'm sure."

"Would you tell me if you did?"

"Yes."

"So again, as a highly trained investigator, I can see how you looked in that picture taken a few years ago, and now I see you standing before me. You are pretty fit now. You can imagine when guys start cheating, or want to cheat that's when it happens. Tell me about it."

"I did not cheat on my wife. Thrive, a product from Le-Vel, helped me. I was 245 lbs."

"You were 245? Wow, you look great man."

"Thank you, and I'm about 180 right now. I have been eating cleaner and Thrive has helped me a lot."

"I've got to imagine, maybe there is a girl that inspired that?"

"No." Chris's answers were unemotional regardless of how personal the questions were becoming.

"Why are you falling out of love?"

"The last five weeks, I was able to be myself again. I couldn't be myself around Shanann."

"Why not?"

"It was like walking on egg shells. I always felt like I was doing something wrong. Does that make sense at all?"

"The timing doesn't make sense to me."

"Okay, but if you can't be yourself around your wife who can you be yourself around?"

"Why can't you be yourself around your wife?"

"I just felt like I'd always have to change who I was. I did everything I could for her and then the last five weeks I was just doing me. One of my buddies said, 'If you can picture your wife with someone else would you get jealous?' At this point I can say no, and he said, 'There's your answer.' If I loved her it would be a different answer."

"When did you start falling out of love?"

"It wasn't the last five weeks. It has been an on-going process for the last year."

"Why?"

"I just didn't feel everything we had when we started dating in 2010, the new relationship spark. You get married and everything is great and then people just fall out of love and that's where I was. Over the last year I thought maybe this is just a phase. You know someone for a long time, and then the spark just isn't there anymore. Maybe you can reignite it somehow, someway. Our conversations weren't the same. When we were apart everything was just short and nothing felt right anymore. The connection wasn't there."

"But why?"

"It wasn't better. I didn't have the passion."

"Why not?"

"I can't tell you. I didn't feel the passion in my heart anymore. I can't give you a definitive answer other than my heart wasn't in it."

"I have to tell you that sounds like a load of horse shit."

"I know."

"What about the girls?"

"Bella and Celeste are the light of my life. I would do anything for those girls. I'd step in front of a bullet or a train for those girls."

"It doesn't add up to me. Why did the spark die?"

"The relationship between me and Shanann has nothing to do with the love I have for these girls. They are the light of my life. I would do anything for them. Shanann and I talked about it. Should we stay together for the kids? If you look it up it doesn't work that way. It might cause more issues for the kids down the road, in their psyche or personality. They see that mom and dad don't sleep in the same room anymore."

"What's going on?" Agent Coder was short and direct with his questions. Tension was building in the room. The clock seemed louder, tick, tick, tick. He continued, "If you had to guess, why two people who are hot and heavy, with kids that they love, what happened?"

"You can't factor in the kids. The love you have for your kids is exponential. I mean it will never die. Those are your kids. The love will never die. Between you and your wife, the love that you have for each other from beginning to end, that type of relationship, when you're in it for that long, something happens. Conversations change, attractions change. When you can put your forehead to someone else's and you know what that person is thinking, that's a connection. I didn't have that connection anymore."

"What do I do to help you walk out of this room and not look like the person who is responsible?" Agent Coder asked.

"You have to trust me when I tell you that I did nothing to these two beautiful girls and I did nothing to my beautiful wife. You have to trust me! I know you don't know me as a person. You've only been around me for like two-and-a-half, three hours. I don't know what your opinion is, but you have to realize that these two beautiful girls and my wife; I had nothing to do with their disappearance. They vanished. They were taken. Someone has taken them. They are safe somewhere. We don't know. I had nothing to do with this act of evil cruelty here. My love for these two girls and my wife; I don't want anything to happen to them. I never have. Whether my wife and I separated or not, I have never wished harm on anyone, on any human being in general. I want them to just run through that front door and just bear tackle me, knock me to the floor, bust my head open. I don't care. The love I have for my family will never die. I want them back. I have to have them back."

"Tell me about a normal day in your house," Agent Coder continued. "You mean one when I'm actually home all day?"

"Pick a school day."

"I get up about 4:00 am and go down and work out for an hour or so. About 5:00 I make some breakfast, eggs or cottage cheese. Everyone is still sleeping. I make CeCe's milk. Bella is iffy about milk in the morning so I fill up the water bottles and put them in the fridge. I make sure the backpacks have a change of clothes, their hats, water shoes and sunscreen if it is a swim day. I make sure all of that is in their back packs."

"Change of clothes for what?"

"In case they have an accident, not so much Bella, but for Celeste. I make sure they have their little 'binkies' for their naps. I have all that laid out and then I go to work. The kids dictate when Shanann wakes up. Bella usually goes in and lays in bed with her. Celeste joins them and they watch cartoons for a while. About 6:30 they get up. Shanann gets ready, showers, does her makeup, takes the kids to their rooms and gets them ready for school. Bella has a school uniform. CeCe doesn't have one yet. They go downstairs and have breakfast. CeCe has cereal, but Bella likes cinnamon toast. They might have a snack, dry cereal I put in the car, and they go to school. They stay at school until about 4:15. I am usually home by then and can go pick them up. I sign them out. They always want mommy after a long day of school. Shanann will have something for the girls that they want, maybe pizza, or French fries. They wash their hands, sit at the table, and eat their dinner. I take them upstairs and give them a shower, lotion them up, put their pajamas on and we go back downstairs, and have a little nighttime snack like cheese-its. About, 6:30, they get their medicine, and they watch a cartoon on their little couches until 7:00 pm. Then they go upstairs and brush their teeth. CeCe gets an overnight diaper. Bella doesn't and we read a book. CeCe wants the tiger book. We growl at the last part and then turn their rain machines on. We give them both a kiss good night. CeCe wants me to put her to bed. Bella wants Shanann to put her to bed. We close the door, night-night!"

"Can we talk about the morning they disappeared? We already talked a bit. 4:00 a.m. the alarm and then prep until 4:15? Then this challenging talk starts. You then leave around 5:30 to go to work. What was your day like?"

"I went out to oil locations until 12:10 pm. That's when I got the doorbell visitor notification."

"What do you do out there?"

"I operate the oil and gas locations we have. Maintenance or inspections, get them running again."

"Are you the guy with the wrench or the boss?"

"I'm one of the field coordinators. We direct the day."

"Which location did you go to at 5:30?

I went to the Cervi 319 Allen Ranch, first, and stayed there about an hour. I then went to the 1129, on the same ranch for 20 minutes, doing an inspection.

Then I went to the 1029 and was there most of the day doing maintenance.

"Were there people with you?

"Yeah, I gave their names to the police. I texted home at 7:40 to see where Shanann was. I was also trying to call my foreman and wasn't getting phone service out there." Chris sat silent.

"So let's have the hard conversation again. How old are they?" Agent Coder dug in again.

"CeCe is three and Bella will be five in December."

"You can imagine the more time that goes by, the harder and harder it will be to find your girls, to find clues? The weather will be a factor, and clues may start blowing away. Everything is going to disappear. And every day that goes by, we will be looking for the man who did this, and you can imagine that we are going to include you as that man, so let's talk about that. I think that you are trying to put on a brave face because you're a man, and you're a father, and you're a husband. I can tell that there's something you are not telling me. I'm not sure what it is and I don't know why that is. There is something that is making you a little bit uncomfortable. I just don't believe some of the things you're telling me, okay? I simply do not believe you."

"What have I said that makes you not believe me at all?" Chris asked.

"This just doesn't make sense to me. It doesn't add up. Can we talk about two Chris's? The tale of two Chris's? You need to help me know which Chris I am looking at today and which Chris you really are. Chris number one is right here. He fell out of love with his wife. He started wondering what it might be like if he didn't have a wife or girls to take care of. He spent some time alone and liked that time alone. He came home. He may or may not have had a conversation about how to get out of this marriage or how to fix it, most likely how to get out of it. He is looking at a bachelor pad in Brighton, and did something terrible to his wife and kids that may have been an accident. I think it was an accident. That's not the Chris I'm looking at right now."

"The Chris you're looking at right now is a man who loved these kids and loves his wife and will never, never, do anything to harm them. That's the Chris you're looking at right now. The Chris you're looking at wants these kids and his wife back at his house right now. That is the Chris you are looking at," Chris explained.

"Why didn't you call 911 when you thought they were missing?"

"I didn't think anything was wrong," Chris responded in a shaky voice, finally showing emotion.

"I think you knew what was wrong."

"I did not know what was wrong, sir!" Chris stated defiantly. "I promise you that!"

"What do you think it's going to look like when someone finds out it was not you that called 911?"

"I suppose they have their own perception about what's going on here, but I know my wife. I know that sometimes she doesn't text me back. I know that happens." Chris was tired of the relentless questioning over the long hours. He continued, "This has happened multiple times. If she is busy with work she doesn't get back to me. That's why it didn't register for me that day."

"Back to the tale of two Chris's? There is a Chris who cares and…" Agent Coder pressed.

"I care, I promise," Chris stated with annoyance.

"Tell me about the call to the day care."

"I called to see if the girls were there and they said they weren't. I told them since they weren't there they should put them back on the waiting list."

"That's not what you told me."

"I told them we are going to sell the house. We're going to put it on the market and probably wouldn't be in the area anymore."

"Those are two different things Chris."

"Well I wanted them to be back on. I put them on the wait list because they weren't there."

"Why weren't they there?"

"I don't know."

"Where were they going to go?"

"Shanann took them to a friend's house."

"Why didn't they go to day care?" Agent Coder asked sternly.

"I'm not sure. Honestly sir, I'm not sure."

"It's hard for me as a father to talk about this," Agent Coder admitted.

"I know."

"Not because it's a hard issue to talk about. It's because I'm worried about your daughters under your care."

"You don't have to worry about them under my care. I watched them all weekend. I went to a pool party at a friend's house. I love those kids with all my heart. Nothing in this world would ever make me do anything to these kids or my wife."

"When you walk out of here, there is nothing I can say to a room full of police officers that is going to convince them that you had nothing to do with this."

"I know."

"You know what they think? Here's a guy who didn't call 911, who woke his wife up at a ridiculous hour because he was so guilty about something that he had to get it off his chest, to say I don't love you anymore, I'm leaving. That didn't go well. Okay so what happened?"

"She told me she wanted me to wake her up before I left. I didn't just wake her up to tell her that." Chris spoke forcefully, "I woke her up and we talked. Usually at 4:00 in the morning I go downstairs and work out, but I wanted to talk to her about this."

Chris continued, "I love these girls. I love these girls so much, and this picture right here. Celeste and Bella are my life. I helped make those kids. There's nothing in my life that means more to than these kids. Nothing! Kids are your lifeline. They come first. Kids, spouse, family. That's what it has always been," Chris's voice was emotional when he spoke of Bella and CeCe.

"Nothing you've told me tonight makes sense, nothing. Nothing you've told me tonight feels like the truth. Can we start over?"

"Sure."

"I think that there's something that happened that got a little out of control.

"There was no fight. There was nothing physical. We didn't raise our voice, nothing! I promise you that, sir. There was nothing physical with this conversation."

"When was the last time you saw with your daughters?"

"I saw them in the monitors as it was switching back and forth."

"When is the last time you saw your wife?"

"She was lying in the bed as I was walking out the bedroom door."

"When we finally get the guy who took them, what do you think we should do?"

"Honestly, they're going to come home safe, correct, when you find the guy?

When we find the guy, they're coming home?" Chris paused nervously before he answered, "Life in prison? That's what I would think with two kids involved."

"What if he hurt them?" Agent Coder pushed.

"I'm not sure. Is the death penalty even used in Colorado? I mean if these kids are not alive there is nothing you can do to help me cope with that. If those kids are not okay."

"All right, what was your plan after you guys separated?"

"Try to get an apartment and we go our separate ways. We would try to sell the house first, of course, before we can do anything. Hopefully we would both get apartments close to one another and do a fifty-fifty thing. I was going on an eight-six schedule in September with six days off. It would be perfect to have the kids half time and she could have them the other half."

"Tonight's been pretty intense, I can imagine. How are you feeling?" Agent Coder asked.

"I slept like two hours last night so I'm burning on empty now," Chris responded. "Why don't we do this? I'm sure you don't mind if we finish this tomorrow. I know you are feeling a little pressure from me."

"That's your job."

"I wouldn't be doing my job if I didn't grill you a little bit."

"Yeah, you seem like two different guys," Chris stated, jokingly. "You are doing your job though."

"Can I make a commitment to you? We aren't going to stop working until we find them. There is going to be a time when you feel this pressure from other people. I'm not the only one who thinks that there is a possibility that you had something to do with this."

"Like another FBI agent?" Chris asked tentatively.

"Everyone! Okay, Chris, have you ever watched the news and they said two girls and a pregnant woman are missing? If that's all you heard what do you think the public thinks?"

"Husband!"

"Husband. I'm going to make a commitment that I am going to be your guy, the one that handles the investigation, and the guy you can come to. Tonight we had to talk about some rough things, but I hope that you know I did that respectfully. I think that you can see that. As we go on, hours or days, I want you to know that I wanted to be in this room tonight. I wanted to talk to you and I hope you will want to talk to me. When you have questions or concerns I want you to call the detective, and I want you to call me. If you think we aren't doing something well enough, I want you to say, 'I have to call Graham or Dave'. When you need a night to yell at somebody or maybe have a good cry, I want you to call me. I can't imagine what you're going through. I just can't."

"Today has been a whirlwind. Yesterday, I thought she was just at someone's house, but today with the drones, the police, the news, it is like a scene out of a movie,"
Chris stated, through his exhaustion.

"It's too much! It's too much for one person to handle. I want to be part of the team that helps you. Tonight when you go home, one of two things is going to happen. You might pass out because you're so tired, but that's probably not what is going to happen. Your head is going to race. Tonight when you lay down you are going to wonder why I asked you certain things. You're going to think, 'screw him how dare he accuse me'.

You're going to say, 'I wonder if they thought of this, and I probably should have told him something, like this or that'. When those thoughts come, I want you to call me or Dave. It is fair for your mind to race, so call me, okay? You need a lifeline. You need someone you can call. I want to be that guy, all right? And I want you to know if I didn't accuse you a little bit you would probably wonder if I was good at my job."

"One of my buddies was straight up with me and said none of this looks good. He said he wasn't going to accuse me, but his wife and friends they won't talk to me right now."

"Okay that is one Chris. Let's talk about the other Chris. He's right here. I can see that you're a good man. You have beautiful daughters that are well clothed and well fed. Children who are unhappy don't smile like this." Agent Coder pointed to the picture of the girls that was lying on the table. "Those are beautiful kids. They have a good dad and I know it."

"The picture on my phone is a better one. I'll show it to you." Chris sounded utterly exhausted.

"Those kids have a good dad who loves them. I was very impressed when I asked you about their day, how involved you are. A lot of dads don't get extra clothes, and cook eggs, and give them snacks at night. For a lot of men that's women's work, but you're not that guy."

"I like to be involved."

"Chris can you look at me for one second? If there is something that happened, it's okay. It really is. If something happened, an accident, something you're afraid to tell me. If there's something that happened between you and your wife, it's okay. You can always tell me and if you want to talk fifteen minutes after you leave, I will answer the phone. If there is something that got out of hand, if there is something you know, I want you to go home and remember that I'm the guy you can talk to. I'm not going to judge you. I have kids. Sometimes I joke with my wife, 'I just need two weeks alone'. When you told me about your five weeks alone, I thought, 'that sounds like a slice of heaven'. Sometimes it is a bit much." Agent Coder paused and then continued, "I still want to organize the search in your house tonight."

"It rained hard tonight. It blew over four trash cans in my yard. Whatever is there, is there." Chris explained.

"I want to talk to you again tomorrow, okay? I want you to get a good night sleep, a good breakfast, a work out, whatever your routine is."

"My dad flies in about 8:00 or 9:00 in the morning."

"Here's what I would love to have happen. Go get your dad. He's going to want to know everything that's happening. He's your dad."

"He's called me like ten times today."

"He is going to have questions, and concerns, and will want to know all of it. I would like for you and me to talk tomorrow, to do a polygraph, and move past all of this. I want to move past wondering what Chris I am talking to. I want to get it all behind us. So, can we say tomorrow at 11:00, we do the polygraph? Let's get that done and move past it. Do you have any questions?"

"Can I have your phone number, so, if I am delayed, I can call?"

"One of the things that makes us wonder which Chris we are talking to, is when you don't answer the phone. I get that you might be busy, but if you go a whole day without answering the phone."

"No that won't happen."

"Can we promise each other we will answer one another?"

"If I'm with my dad, I will definitely call you back."

"I'm going to try to leave you alone tonight, but if something comes up I might need to call you. Some of the things we need to do at the house are better at night, and some in the morning, so we will probably start very early in about three or four hours. Will you not go home? Can you go to your friend's house? I can't tell you not to go home, but I would like for you to not go to the house. Can you just pick up your dad in the morning and come straight here? Let's finish the search. There will be a patrol officer in the front and the back tonight. We also don't want anyone else to be in there. Don't go there without telling us."

Another agent entered the room. "We have been getting calls all night. There is a sighting at Wall-mart. We have a surveillance picture. Is this your daughter?" The agent showed Chris the picture, and he shook his head no.

Chris was incredibly relieved to leave the room, the questions, and his new best friend?

Agent Coder ended with a notation on the recorder: "End of recording 11:06 pm. Tuesday August, 14th.

Chapter 6

Shanann couldn't shake her anxiety. It felt like she had been searching for Bella for hours, for days. Why was this happening? Why couldn't she just take her daughter and go with Gran? She missed the girls so much, and she had a deep longing to hold Nico, to feel his velvet skin once again. The anxiety of her loss was overwhelming. Shanann didn't want to lose herself in grief or despair, but she wasn't sure how to overcome this situation.

Okay think. In the past, Shanann controlled anxiety with organization. When everything was in its place, she felt secure, safe. She hated chaos, a lack of control. She needed perfection. *Labels!* Whenever she had anxiety she would organize and label everything. Shanann went into her very neat kitchen. Everything was meticulously labeled. Shanann began tearing the labels off of her spices. They looked old and dusty. Yes, she needed new fresh labels. She went to her label maker and began the tedious process of making new ones. She would make a new label for every container in her kitchen. The idea sparked a sense of purpose. She needed a project, something to take her mind off of everything. This had always worked for her. She worked for what seemed like hours. Her kitchen counter was covered with the old torn labels as she fashioned new ones. She strategically placed them in their proper place. Cinnamon, sugar, coffee, tea, cloves, whole wheat flour, almond flour, coconut flour, etc. *Perfection!* They were clean, fresh, organized!

The cookie jar. The girls loved the ceramic keeper of the sacred cookie treasure. Shanann smiled at the thought of their beautiful little smiles as she would take the lid off and dig deep for their favorite snack. She made a perfect label for it, a very special one for her baby girls. She lovingly put the label on the jar. *No, it's crooked.* She pulled it off and made another one. She very carefully attached the label in the strategic location. *Perfect! Damn, it is still crooked. How is that possible?* She tried several more times to create and attach a perfect label in a perfect location, on a perfect cookie jar. *Crooked! Oh my God, this is ridiculous!* Shanann's anxiety and anger at her inability to complete this simple task was reaching a boiling point. *Okay, one more time.* Shanann made the label and very carefully put it in its place. *No fucking way. Crooked!* Shanann took the cookie jar and threw it across the kitchen. It exploded into a million pieces. A ceramic nightmare scattered across her clean floor. She dropped to the floor and began to sob.

How could you, Chris? How could cheat on me? How could you be so angry with me? I wanted things to be perfect for us, for our family. I wanted to be perfect for you. I wanted you to be perfect for me and the girls. Shanann spoke the works out loud. Then she screamed them at the top of her lungs, "We were making a perfect life!"

The sound of her words filled the room, echoing off of the high ceilings and reverberating across the cold floor she was lying on. She was exhausted. Striving for perfection was too much fucking work. Shanann got up, left her labels, left her shattered mess, and left her expectations of perfection. She went outside to breathe.

Speaks With Stars was sitting in his usual spot, cross-legged on the grass. Shanann had no idea what time of day or night it was until she saw the sky. The sun was setting and the view took her breath away. Pink and purple splashes mingled with scattered flecks of gold filtering through soft wisps of blue, weaving in between hazy billows of fluff. Mountain peaks reached up to meet the lofty canvas of color and translucent light. A gentle breeze lifted the scent of pine and wild roses. Shanann sat down beside Speaks With Stars. His presence was calming and she welcomed the smell of sage and burning wood. Shanann took a deep breath and rested in the peaceful view of the setting sun.

Speaks With Stars smiled slightly at Shanann before he offered her the pipe he was smoking. She hesitated. *Smoking is deadly, it causes yellowing of the teeth, and secondhand smoke is bad for the kids.* Suddenly, as if rebelling against her own thoughts, Shanann took the pipe and inhaled deeply. She immediately began coughing and choking profusely. Then it hit her. A deep calm began creeping through her body, and every muscle eased into a gentle state of relaxation. Shanann realized they were no longer sitting in her front yard. They were sitting on a very steep cliff, surrounded by mountainous rocks that seemed to reach to the sky. Green pines filtered in between the crevices, easing their way to the valley floor. Shanann was mesmerized by the magnitude and grandeur of the place. Speaks With Stars sensed her awe.

"This is my favorite place in the world," he shared.

Shanann was overcome with gratitude that she was his honored guest. She wanted to share something with him. They sat in silence for many moments, reveling in the beauty of this sacred spot. "I broke the cookie jar," Shanann suddenly blurted out.

Speaks With Stars just sat staring into the abyss, taking in the wonder of the view.

"I didn't just break it, I obliterated it," Shanann continued, looking into the mystery of the cliffs.

Speaks With Stars offered her the pipe. She took it, with minor hesitation, and took a smaller hit this time. She managed to muffle the anticipated, less intense cough.

Shanann was stunned that she was not worried about the thousand-foot drop that was less than five feet from them. She was smoking something that made her body feel like a noodle.

"I threw it across the room and it exploded," Shanann said with satisfaction, right before she giggled.

Speaks With Stars sat silently, absorbing the energy that pulsed though the rocks. He felt a deep connection with the birds as they soared with unimaginable freedom, and his thoughts lingered in the never-ending sky. A cool breeze blew through his long dark hair, gently swaying the feathers in his braid. Suddenly, as if coming out of a deep trance, he looked over at Shanann. His eyes were wide with wonder. He sensed that his young friend had experienced a groundbreaking revelation, but he was a bit confused. His voice was deep as it echoed into the valley, "What's a cookie jar?"

Shanann smiled the width of the valley, and rested her head on his shoulder.

Chapter 7

The night had been agonizing. Chris thought staying with Nick and Amanda would make things easier but he still had an incredibly long, restless, night. His dad would be at the airport at 9:00 a.m. It would be good to see him, but Chris was not looking forward to the questions Ronnie would undoubtedly ask.

The ride to the airport was long due to traffic. Chris was relieved when he saw his father. Ronnie Watts was a tall man of large stature. His white hair and a white mustache suited him well against his tanned, weathered skin. His sunglasses were tucked into the V-neck of his short sleeve light blue polo shirt. He gave a Chris a big hug when he saw him. Chris immediately saw the deep concern in his father's eyes. They exchanged small-talk about the flight and the weather. When they were in the car Chris explained that he was going right to the police station to take a polygraph. Ronnie took the news in stride and told Chris he wanted to come along.

"I might be there a long time dad," Chris warned.

"It's okay son."

The ride was easier than Chris anticipated. Instead of talking about Shanann and the girls and what was obviously going on, Ronnie engaged Chris in a lengthy conversation about sports. Chris appreciated the gesture. He was already weary of the flood of drama that now surrounded him. Chris and Ronnie had always been in tuned with one another even if they didn't frequently have heart-to-heart conversations. Emotion wasn't always the most comfortable path in the Watts' household when Chris was growing up. They arrived at the station, and Chris was escorted back into the small claustrophobic room where he anticipated that he would spend a good deal of the day. Ronnie would wait for him in the main reception area. While Chris appreciated his dad being so close, he felt guilty that Ronnie would probably be waiting a long time.

Agent Graham Coder entered the room with another agent.

Graham proceed to address Chris, "As we mentioned yesterday we wanted to knock out the polygraph. Why don't we do that now? This is Tammy. Did you meet her yesterday?" Graham asked Chris.

"No, I didn't," Chris answered.

"Hi Chris, how are you?" Colorado Bureau of Investigations agent Tammy Lee, greeted Chris in a very friendly manner. She wore a striped, navy and white long sleeve sweater over a blue shirt. Her short blondish, brown hair was parted on the side, and she had the appearance of a first grade teacher. The small clock was the only thing that interfered with the sterile white walls. While the room was very unfriendly, Tammy and Graham seemed welcoming. Graham jumped right in to the conversation.

"When we're done we can figure out our game plan. Does your dad have the availability to use the car in case we are here for a while?" Graham asked.

"Yeah he can drive, but he won't know where to go since he can't go to the house. He can go to my friend's house. I don't know if I'll be here an hour or maybe longer," Chris said with high hopes. He wanted to leave and take his dad for a BBQ sandwich at *Georgia Boys*.

"Do you want me to go talk to him and let him know what's going on? He can go grab a bite to eat or something. And I'll go give your dad the keys and we'll get him set up," Graham offered.

"I've been getting text messages from the media. Not just here, but from the *Today Show* and *Good Morning America*. I don't know what to do about that," Chris explained.

"Well, I think that you can certainly do whatever you want, but let's knock this out, get back to the team, and then we'll make a plan," Graham offered.

"I've been getting different advice. Shanann's mom said if it is a kidnapping I shouldn't talk to the media. I'm torn on what to do. The media is reaching out to my parents, friends, and everyone."

"Okay, while you are doing this you are free to ignore everything else. Let's get the polygraph done and I think it will really clear your mind. Let's put a hold on texting *Good Morning America* and focus on this," Graham suggested.

"I haven't responded to anyone."

Tammy jumped in and addressed Graham, "I'll come get you when we're done. Go ahead and have a seat right here Chris." Graham left the small room, closing the door behind him.

Chris sat down nervously at the end of the table. "I've never done this before."

"I'll explain everything to you. Most people will never take a polygraph in their entire life," Tammy explained.

"Yeah, I don't really know what to expect."

"So how are you feeling today?" Tammy asked.

"Sick to my stomach, honestly. The first day I thought she was just somewhere. After yesterday, with everything going on at the house, it went to the other extreme. I have been checking my phone to see if someone has her, or if she's in trouble."

Tammy addressed Chris, "I think it's totally awesome that you're here today and I commend you. We do this in all of our missing person cases so don't think we are singling you out. In these cases we start from the inside and work our way out. This is one way to clear yourself if you didn't have anything to do with it. That lets everyone know they don't have to waste time focusing on you, and can put all of their attention on Shanann and the girls, and focus on someone else if they need to. My name is Tammy. You can call me Tammy. I'm an agent with Colorado Bureau of Investigation. Anytime a law enforcement agency, a district attorney's office, or the governor needs assistance with a case, they can call the CBI. In this type of case they are calling in all of the resources they can. They asked me if I would come here, chat with you, clear you up, and get you on your way. This polygraph will be recorded. There is a camera up there and a digital backup recording I am doing. This will take a couple of hours. You will get the same polygraph I gave to someone last week. It is very structured and you will know all of the questions I am going to ask before you even take the polygraph. I lot of people think they will be hooked up and asked a bunch of random questions, and of course they will react poorly to that. It doesn't work like that, at all. Obviously you are probably nervous, and I would think there was something wrong if you weren't nervous. Even if you don't have anything to hide, it is nerve racking. I have a lot of experience. I went to one of the best schools in the country, and I want you to feel confident that if you didn't have anything to do with this we will find that out today. I have the best training they offer in the United States. We use the most validated testing. That should give you some confidence that you will be cleared today. Nervousness or anxiety cannot fail a polygraph."

"That's how I thought it worked," Chris said nervously.

"No, there are only two ways you can fail a polygraph. The first way would be if you fail to follow my instructions. I am going to give you a lot of instructions, how to sit still, how to answer the questions. If you fail to follow those instructions you will not pass the test. The second way would be if you chose to lie to me today. This is about 100% truth. Even if there is something you didn't tell the investigators since Monday that is totally fine. You can't remember everything. So as long as you are completely honest today, you'll be fine. If you did have something to do with their disappearance it would be really stupid for you to take the polygraph today. You should not be here sitting in this chair if you had anything to do with Shanann and the girl's disappearance. I don't know much about the case. It is Bella and Celeste right?"

"I call her CeCe too, in case it comes up."

"I don't know a lot of the details you have already given. I want you to tell me like you are telling someone for the very first time. Obviously Chris, you are not under arrest. I have no plans to arrest you. If you decide at any time you want to leave today the door is right there. Even after all of these components are attached you can leave if you decide you don't want to continue. Just please let me detach my components before you drag my $6,000 instrument and run out of here." Chris and Tammy both chuckled. He appreciated her easing the tension in the room.

Tammy continued, "It is kind of a maze back here and I will show you the way out if you decide to leave. The door does need to be closed because noise affects the unit. I will read you your rights today. The components are a bit restrictive. They go around your chest and you may feel like you're not free to leave but at any point you are free to go. We are going to go over the rights and the consent form. There is also a medical form to make sure you are physically able to take the test. A lot of people are really nervous before they come in and they smoke weed or take medication. Some people hear voices, and all of those things keep me from giving the polygraph. You seem very lucid, and you're not jittery or moving around. After that we are going to discuss the reason you are here. I want you to tell me everything. We are going to start from the beginning, like I am a friend. You just came to talk, and lay out everything you remember about what happened to Shanann and the girls. We will go over all of the questions. I want you to feel very comfortable about how you are going to answer them. We will do a practice test," Tammy continued to explain in great detail every step of the polygraph.

"You're not working today right?" Tammy asked.

"No."

"Do you have a return date?"

"No."

"How long have you worked for Anadarko?"

"Since January 2015, about three and a half years."

"Do you like it there?"

"Oh yeah, I worked for a contract company before that, and I worked for Ford for eleven years as a technician."

"Oh, so does that translate into your Anadarko stuff?"

"It's mechanical. I like to fix things. When I moved out here, I worked at Ford and I moved up, but then I kind of plateaued. I had carpal tunnel on both of my hands and it was bad. It was just the onset. I didn't need surgery or anything, but now it's so much better. There are a lot of repetitive things in oil and gas, but it isn't as bad as the car industry."

"Are you a worker bee or are you a boss?"

"A little of both. I'm a field operator." Chris went into a lengthy explanation of his work duties. Talking about work for a few minutes was comforting.

Tammy continued bringing Chris back to the room and her questions. "If I mispronounce your wife's name forgive me."

"Just think of shenanigans. That's the way she tells people."

"Does her family call her that?"

"They spelled it as Shan-Ann but she just says Shanann. She was named after Sha-na-na."

Tammy proceeded with the paper work. She read through the form and then read Chris his rights. "You have the right to remain silent. Anything you say can and will be used against you in a court of law. You have the right to talk to a lawyer and have them present with you while you are being questioned. If you cannot afford to hire a lawyer one will be appointed to represent you during questioning if you wish," Tammy continued, asking Chris if he agreed and understood. He proceeded to answer in the affirmative and signed the document. They continued with small talk about the Denver Nuggets and North Carolina college basketball.

"Did you go to college Chris?"

"No, I wish I did. I went to NASCAR Tech in North Carolina, a mechanical school." Chris spoke in detail about the school.

"Do you go by any other names?" Tammy asked.

"Just Chris, but I do have a couple of nicknames. Some people call me Rain-man at work. I can go out to an oil sight once and I'll remember it. When I was young my grandma used to quiz me on the state capitals. I went over to her house every morning before school, and later she would cook me lunch and things like that."

"Have you talked to Shanann's parents at all? Are they coming here?"

"I'm not sure yet. My dad came out for support. He just got here this morning."

Tammy explained the consent form for the polygraph that she would need Chris to sign before she began. They exchanged more small talk and Chris explained how he and Shanann met some of their friends through the Le-Vel business.

"I really don't know what it is or how it works," Tammy confessed.

"It is vitamins and minerals, all plant based, non GMO. It is really healthy for you. You take two pills when you wake up, drink a shake, and then put a patch on. It opens up your pores a little bit and your skin absorbs it. Shanann has me signed up as part of her team, but I don't sell. She says I say too much about the product instead of having them call her. There is one person I work with that uses Thrive."

Tammy continued to engage in small talk with Chris. She asked for his address, and phone number. Reading from his driver's license she mentioned his weight. He explained that he had gained more weight than Shanann when she was pregnant with the girls.

"When you were growing up who did you live with?" Tammy asked.

"My mom, dad, and my sister Jamie."

"Have you spoken with your sister?"

"Yes, and her husband. She is older than I am by a few years. We were close when we were younger, but then the age made a difference."

"Does Jamie have kids?"

"Yes, they are ten and two. I got to see them recently when I was in North Carolina, August 1st through the 7th."

"So, how did you grow up? Were you religious? Who did the discipline?"

"My dad was a parts manager for car dealership, and mom was a secretary/notary. We went to church regularly, First Baptist. I was the quiet one. I wasn't rebellious like my sister. I pretty much woke up to my mom and sister arguing every day. My dad was the disciplinarian. If my dad ever raised his voice I knew he was serious. The discipline was verbal not physical."

"Did anyone struggle with drug or alcohol abuse?"

"My dad did at one point, but it was after I left home. My sister moved in and out of the house a few times. When I left, after high school, I was totally self-sufficient and I never moved back. That seemed to hit him pretty hard. He is my hero, my best friend."

"So you didn't move back home? Did you have any girlfriends at that time?"

"I did have one girlfriend, but nothing serious until I met Shanann in 2010. We got married in 2012. We met through my cousin's wife."

"I need to ask you some of the medical questions. How would you describe your physical condition?"

"Good."

"No major surgeries or accidents?"

"No."

"What did you have for dinner last night? Did you eat?"

"I had pizza after I left Agent Coder at about 11:00. I went to bed at 12:30, and got up about 5:00. About 7:30 this morning I had a protein shake."

"Were you able to sleep last night?"

"Not great."

"Do you drink?"

"Once in a while. I only have one or two beers when I do drink."

Tammy asked a few more questions about Chris's mechanical training, and he explained that if he could do it over he would have studied the technology.

"I have a good math aptitude and I like that aspect of the work. I started as an operator/rover, and I'm now a field operator," Chris explained.

"Okay, now let's discuss the reason you are here. Start from the beginning like we just met and you are telling me about your life."

"In 2010 we met on Facebook. Our first date was a movie theater. I didn't know what I was walking into. There was a doorman dressed in a suit and I was in camo shorts. I felt very under dressed. She was dressed all nice. Then we went to a Kidd Rock concert and I made the same mistake again and was underdressed. I won her over when I ran two miles back to the car because I forgot my ID and couldn't get in. I was soaking wet with sweat. It was the middle of the summer in South Carolina. Our next date was at Myrtle Beach. Her lupus was really acting up. She had joint pain and flair ups. Riding back from the beach she laid on me the entire trip, a two and a half hour drive. I let her rest. In 2011, I proposed to her on another beach at night. She was very tired but I wanted to do it. She is OCD organized. Everything is labeled. We were in Colorado when she was planning a wedding for North Carolina. We got married in the Double Tree Hilton Hotel in November. The wedding was amazing. We went to Myrtle Beach for the honeymoon. In 2013, Dec. Bella was born. It took us a while to get pregnant. She bought me a super- charger for my car the weekend Bella was conceived. It was ironic that it happened that weekend. Bella was such a gift. The doctor said Shanann might not be able to conceive. Shanann had a regular pregnancy, although Bella had shoulder dysplasia when she was born. Then we got pregnant with Celeste. When she was born we staged a photo of Bella in the crib with a little eviction notice. Bella was crying like she didn't want to leave her crib. It was really cute. When CeCe was born I was there and Shanann had a midwife. I bonded more easily with Celeste. With Bella I didn't know what I could, or what I should do. I had no idea, and I pretty much just watched. Bella is a mommy's girl. When CeCe was born I knew how to change a diaper. I could do this. I could help a lot more. CeCe's more of a daddy's girl. Whenever she gets in trouble she calls for me. Shanann gets mad if I stick up for her. Shanann doesn't like coddling her. CeCe recently bit Bella and sometimes she hits her. Having them both around, they are like two peas in a pod. Celeste is more of a rambunctious little munchkin. She is either going or sleeping. She is always looking for something to jump off of," Chris fondly reminisced about the beginnings with Shanann and his daughters.

"Is Bella more like you or Shanann?" Tammy inquired.

"Bella is more like me. She is calm and cautious. And then, Shanann told me about the third child. We are trying for a boy and it is a boy. We found out last week. We were both there when we found out. We haven't told anyone yet."

"Were both of the girls born in Colorado?"

"Yeah, they were both born here."

"Did Shanann have any postpartum?"

"No, nothing like that."

"The girls are pretty close together," Tammy pointed out.

"Yeah, about 19 months."

"That is a lot. So why don't you bring me up to when you joined her in North Carolina?"

"We went to the Le-Vel-Thrive trip in San Diego the end of June, on the 26th. When we came home Frank, Shanann's dad, was here watching the kids and then they all flew to North Carolina to spend time with family. Shanann had Thrive business work and some people she wanted to meet up with. We thought the grandparents would have fun with the kids. Celeste's birthday was during that time, July 17th, so it seemed like a great opportunity for a vacation. I missed the birthday party, but I got to Face-time and see it that way. I was working out, running, just keeping the house up. My flight was July 31st. I flew out for the week so I could fly back with them. When I got there I stayed at my in-law's house and then we went to the beach for five days. It was the kid's first time on the beach and they were ecstatic. They loved playing in the sand. It was an awesome trip, watching them react. I also got to see my grandma, my dad's mom. She is in a nursing home. That day her memory was good and she remembered me. Mama lights up when she sees the kids so that was a good day. My dad came and picked me up so I could spend time with my family. August 7th we went to Shanann's parent's house and got everything packed up and ready to go, and we came home that night. I went back to work on the 8th, and then on the 10th Shanann flew out to Arizona. I had the kids Friday, Saturday, and Sunday. Sunday we went to a birthday party for our friend's four-year-old. There was a mini pool and balloon fights. The kids loved it. CeCe put a water balloon in my pocket and smacked it. It was an awesome day! Shanann's plane was delayed that evening. She didn't arrive in Denver until about 2:00 a.m. I saw the notification for the doorbell cam about 2:45 when she got home. She came to bed and then my alarm went off about 4:00. That's when I usually get up and get ready for work. I woke her up after I got ready for work and we had a talk about selling the house. We also talked about a separation. It was an emotional conversation. We were both crying, and after we talked she said that she was going to take the kids to a friend's house later in the day. I went downstairs, loaded my truck, and went to work. Then about 7:40, or so, I hadn't heard from her. I didn't know where she was taking the kids so I asked her to text me and let me know. It is normal for her not to respond to me. She takes care of her business calls first so I wasn't too alarmed that she didn't get back to me. I continued working and then about 12:10 I got the doorbell alert on my phone. Nickole Atkinson was there so I called her and asked what was going on. Nickole said she hadn't heard from Shanann all day, and I thought that was kind of strange. Nickole was pretty concerned that something strange was going on so I came home. Nickole told me the police officer was there and they couldn't get in to check on Shanann because of the interior latches. The keypad on the garage door doesn't work and they had to wait until I got there to get in. Her car was there, and the car seats were there, so we checked inside the house. Her purse was there and I found her wedding ring. The girls were gone and the house was like a ghost town. Nothing made any sense. There were no clues as to what happened. Her friends were calling me and everyone was reaching out, trying to find her. Detective Baumhover came and asked Nickole and me some questions. Then we went over to the neighbors. He has a security camera facing my driveway. It picked up a few different angles. I watched it but there was no video of Shanann leaving the front, at all. I was at a loss for words. She wouldn't just leave everything here. Even the kid's meds were still there. The girl's blankets were gone. They talked to the other neighbors to see if anyone else had video, but they didn't. They were going house-to-house, and there were no clues anywhere. At this point I was just hoping they were safe. I was calling the hospitals, and hotels, and nothing. That night I had every light in the house on. I lay in bed, but I couldn't sleep. A few friends came by. I don't know how or why this happened. I kept waiting for a phone call, from a number that wasn't familiar, hoping it was Shanann and she was some place safe with the girls. I kept hoping for a knock on the door, hoping the kids would just run in. That didn't happen. I was trying to process everything. I miss the kids sitting at the dinner table, even throwing their chicken nuggets at me. I went to their rooms. I wanted to turn their rain machines on and read them a book. I wasn't giving them their meds or nighttime snack. It just hit me. I don't need to turn the monitor on because they aren't here. Where are they? Then I didn't even want to stay in the house, but I knew

I needed to in case they came to the front door. I just lay in bed, took phone calls, and couldn't sleep. The next day when everything started happening, the news crews, the dogs, the police, it sets in that my worst fear was being realized. I thought she was with someone and she was safe, but the whole scene took me in a totally different direction. Our friends started coming by to show their support. I didn't want to be alone, at all. I just want to find them. I hope they are safe, wherever they are. FBI agent Graham has been really helpful. I hope they are okay, I mean not being able to tuck them in at night. I mean, we made those kids. Just hearing, 'I love you daddy, or I miss you daddy' meant everything. They were without me for five weeks. It's a nightmare."

"Thanks for explaining that to me. I have more questions. You kept saying you thought Shanann was at a friend's house. Do you still think that?"

"I don't think so now. Maybe she is at a hotel or with someone, I don't know. I just want her to be safe. With everything that is going on now, I feel like maybe someone has her, someone who isn't keeping her safe, or something terrible has happened and that's the nightmare."

"And what would that terrible thing be?"

"That somebody hurt them."

"And that's running through your mind?"

Chris was becoming more emotional, "I don't want that running through my mind but it is. I want them to come home."

"We want them to come home. So let's take this back to when Shanann went to Arizona. Why did she go?"

"It was a Le-Vel-Thrive conference. There was a lot of training involved."

"Did she make a lot of money with the company?"

"Yeah, she did really well."

"You said you kind of talk about separation when you woke her up. When did all of that start?"

"When she was in North Carolina and I was back here. When we were calling and texting we felt disconnected."

"Before June, going back, were their issues?" Tammy asked.

"Even a year ago I could see that it wasn't going to be as hot and heavy as when we first met. You know that spark just wasn't the same. Marriages have their lows and highs, and I was hoping that things would work themselves out. When the kids are involved it's even harder. We put of lot of focus on the kids. We didn't go out on dates or anything like that. We put our attention on the kids. I think we lost something. We didn't have those deep conversations anymore. When she was in North Carolina it just felt short and disconnected. When I got out there the kids ran though the airport to greet me, but I felt like something was missing between Shanann and I. And when I was there we talked a little bit, but usually texted our feelings about what was going on. Everyone was there and we weren't really alone. The texts were about where the relationship was going. We were bringing a third kid into this world. What is the relationship going to look like? Are we going to work this out? Or will this lead to a separation? Will we be civil for the kids, but not work on the relationship anymore?"

"What was her reaction to all of that?"

"It was emotional, a lot of crying. I'm not sure how to explain that, but it was more of how are we going to make this work."

"She wanted to make it work?"

"We both wanted to make it work, but are we at a point where we can make it work? When she went to Arizona she confided in her friends about our relationship, that we were having difficulties."

"In North Carolina, was that the first time you guys talked about not staying together and was that you more than Shanann? Did you bring it up to her?"

"Yeah, that was me bringing it up to her. I didn't feel the connection anymore. I don't feel like I used to. I can't see myself in this anymore."

"And she said what?"

"She really didn't know what to say. She wanted to fix things, maybe go to counseling or read a self-help book or something. We both wanted to work on it. Bringing a new kid into the world, we wanted the environment to be as healthy as possible."

"Did you sleep in the same bed in North Carolina?" Tammy's questions were becoming more and more personal yet she seemed non-assuming and Chris felt comfortable answering.

"I slept in the kid's room once and then on the couch?"

"When you were in North Carolina did you have sex, or were you affectionate?"

"No, not really. It wasn't really there."

"Before North Carolina did you have a healthy sex life?"

"The last time we had sex, up to that point, was when the kid was conceived, sometime in May."

"When you had sex in May, was it a date, or a special time?"

"We had been talking about having another kid and she was ovulating."

"Did she track that?"

"Yeah, she always knew. She had a cycle tracker."

"So did you feel like sex was more like a job, or did you really enjoy it?"

"No, it was never just to get pregnant, but you do have to kind of work around the cycle."

"Before that time, in May, how often were you having sex?"

"Maybe once or twice a week."

"So why did it significantly stop after she conceived?"

"There were times when we went a month or two without having sex. Sometimes I would try and she was too tired, or she was aggravated by something. I was usually the one who initiated it, but that is just married life." Chris slightly laughed. "You keep trying. You never stop trying, but if you felt like it was a job, or a task you wouldn't want to try. I enjoyed our sex life."

"In North Carolina, when you were talking about separating, did she accuse you of seeing anyone else?"

"That did come up, but I reminded her of the kind of guy I am, that I wouldn't do that. My friend has said that he could send his wife with me for a week and he could trust that nothing would ever happen. People know the kind of guy I am. I'm not the kind of guy who would take advantage of the fact that my wife was gone for five weeks. I respect her and she respects me. If she is somewhere safe right now, I don't think it is with a guy. I mean, if it she is, it would be fine. I want her and the kids to be safe and if they're with another guy, who is keeping them safe, fine. We'll talk about that later. I never had an inkling she would cheat on me."

"So how did that come up?"

"We were just distant with each other, and sometimes when she called, I would be out for a run and wouldn't answer her right away. Sometimes she could tell that I just wanted to go work out."

"Did she accuse you of doing other things?"

"She knew I was out. She had no reason to have that fear in her head, but being away for that long, and being pregnant, she had those fears."

"How was she different when she wasn't pregnant?"

"She was just more emotional. She was with her mom, who is full Italian, and always gung-ho about everything, and it would make Shanann really anxious sometimes. It was a lot of stress being with her family and my family. And she was there with the kids which is stressful."

"Do you all get along? You said you went to see your folks by yourself. Was there a reason she didn't join you?"

"Well, there was an incident where my mom had something in the house that CeCe was allergic to, ice cream. CeCe's allergic to tree nuts, and kiwi. My mom had ice cream that CeCe couldn't have and my mom let my sister's kid eat next to CeCe. She is the kind of kid who might just lunge at the ice cream, and Shanann felt like it was dangerous for her. CeCe had just a sliver of a cashew one time that made her react. That kind of drove Shanann to say the kids couldn't come over if my mom had that stuff in the house. So when I got there my folks hadn't seen the kids in two weeks. Shanann said the kids couldn't go over to see my folks."

"How did you feel about that?"

"I was hurt. I wanted my parents to see their grandbabies. When I went over there I wanted to bring the kids, but I respected her decision. I really wanted to see my parents, my sister, and her family."

"Did Shanann tell any of her family about the potential separation?"

"No, she didn't."

"How do you know?"

"She told me she wasn't going to tell her parents."

"Did you guys talk about counseling?"

"Yes, on the 8th right before she left for Arizona. I didn't really think we needed to go to counseling. Anything we were saying could be said without counseling. We didn't have to go to somewhere, but she wanted to go. I was open, but didn't really want to do it. I would have if she thought it would help. I didn't think it would work."

"What was the relationship like when she left for Arizona?

"We knew what the sex of the baby was. We were going to tell everyone when she got back. Nickole picked her up and we hugged goodbye. Friday the kids and I hung out. We ran errands."

"Did you talk to Shanann that night? Did you face-time with the girls?"

"No, we don't do that. The girls would get really upset. Bella was already asking for her a lot. There was no contact between her and the kids when she was gone. She can't talk to the girls when she goes out of town. It would be like a cry-fest for all of them. They really miss her."

"How do you chill out? Did you have anyone over?"

"No, Saturday I played with the girls. We couldn't go to the park, they were doing construction there."

"What happened in the evening?"

"One of our neighbor's daughters, McKenna, watched the girls. I went to a Rockies game."

"Who did you go with?"

"People from work."

"Who did you go with from work?" Tammy pressed.

"Cody. It was a work function, and Sam."

"What time did you leave for the game?"

"Around 5:00. The game started at 6:10."

"Did you stop to eat dinner?"

"Yeah, at the Lazy Dog."

"Who did you eat dinner with?"

"The same people. I came home about 11:00. I stopped by the Conoco and got some cash to pay the sitter."

"How did you get there?"

"The Lexus."

"Did you pick up anyone on the way?"

"No."

"Did you just meet them down there?"

"Yeah."

"Do you and the people you work with get together often?"

"No, this was just a random thing. I never win anything. I won a ticket."

"All three of you won tickets?"

"Yeah."

"And did anyone else meet you there?"

"No, it was just a random thing."

"When you were at the game did you mention anything to your co-workers about what is going on with Shanann?"

"Oh lord no!" Chris stated emphatically. "I didn't want anyone at work to know anything about my personal life. I did talk to my foreman a bit. I just wanted him to be aware that we were thinking of a separation, and if he thought my mind was not on task he should tell me or send me home. There is so much pressure at work you need to be fully on the task. It is pretty dangerous. He was pretty supportive."

"So, then on Sunday you went to the birthday party, and the girls played with the water balloons. What happened when you came home?"

"I put them in the shower. They had sand all over them from the sandbox, and then they wanted cold pizza for dinner. It was left over from McKenna babysitting them. Then they got in their nightgowns and got ready for bed."

"What did their nightgowns look like?"

"CeCe had a pink one with a drawing of a bird, and Bella's said something like 'believe' on it. Then we face-timed Shanann's parents. They talked for a while and they sat on their little couches. CeCe has a Minnie Mouse couch and Bella has a Sophia couch. They had a snack. Then they brushed their teeth and went to bed. The rain machines were on, and they usually stay in bed, but Bella came out twice and asked for her mom. I told her she wasn't there yet, but she would be home in the morning. Shanann wouldn't want to go in and wake them up. Celeste didn't come out."

"Did you talk to Shanann and send her pics or anything while she was gone?"

"Yeah, I sent pics of the girls and we communicated during the weekend. We just texted about ordinary things."

"If you could have taken her pulse, then, did she seem like herself? Or was she upset?"

"It was hard to tell through her texts, but I knew she was ready to get home and see the girls."

"How did your relationship seem?"

"I could tell she was ready to be home, to see us all. She had only been home for two days in six weeks and she was really ready to be there. Her flight was delayed and she texted me then, and then I felt her getting into bed around 2:00 a.m."

"Did you hear her when she got home?

"I felt her get into the bed."

"What is Shanann's routine when she comes to bed?"

"Normally she'll brush her teeth and use a makeup remover. She takes something for her stomach. Then she'll lay in bed and make phone calls, if she needs to. She charges her apple watch and her phone. She wears a tee shirt and underwear to bed."

"Was there hugging or kissing when she climbed into the bed?"

"No, I just felt that she was there."

"Does she wear jewelry?"

"Her wedding ring. The only time she takes if off is to color her hair."

"Was her ring left in the house?" Tammy asked.

"Yes."

"Is that unusual?"

"Yes, very! She colored her hair last week and even when she does she puts her ring right back on."

"So when she got into bed was there a conversation?"

"No, but she told me the night before that she wanted to get up early and get the 'airport off of her', you know clean up and shower!"

"She wanted to get up in two hours?" Tammy asked, smiling.

"She told me that when we thought her plane was still on time and she would have been in at 11:00."

"Did you think she still wanted to get up when you were getting ready for work?"

"If I assumed that she didn't want to get up I knew I'd be in trouble. I've assumed many times and it didn't work out. You don't want to make her mad."

"So how did you wake her up?" Tammy asked.

"I just kind of lightly rubbed her shoulder, because she'll give me the alligator eye, like one eye open, one eye shut, like what the hell are you doing? So I just gently rubbed her shoulder to wake her up slowly."

"So were you out of the bed when you woke her up?"

"I jumped back into the bed. I was on top of the covers. I asked her if she wanted to get up and shower. And then I asked if we could talk a little bit. And she said yeah, let's talk."

"Was she groggy at all?"

"She was pretty with it, surprisingly, but she was pretty with it."

"And how did you start that conversation?"

"I told her we need to sell this house. We need to downsize. We need to get something less expensive, so we aren't strapped so much. We are paying $2,700 a month on the mortgage. With the kid's school and medical bills, that's a lot. She had already contacted a realtor the week before so they knew we were interested. Maybe we could do something smaller, like Brighton or Northglenn, something cheaper. I didn't want to talk about a separation in a phone call, or something like that. We needed to be face-to-face to talk about that."

"So tell me more about how that conversation went."

"I told her I didn't feel a connection anymore. The love we had in the beginning, I don't feel that anymore. She was crying and it was emotional and…"

"Were you mad at all?"

"We were both crying, but that comes with a conversation like that."

"Did she accuse you of anything?"

"I mean, being a woman, she asked if there was anyone else and I told her there wasn't. I said, 'This is me talking to you. It's not like someone came into my life and took me from you. This is just me talking to you'. There is no outside influence."

"Did she believe that?"

"Yeah, I mean I believe she would never have an affair, and she knows I would never do that. We talked about that before."

"Did she ever accuse you of that in the past?"

"No!" Chris stated adamantly.

"Did she ever suspect anyone that you were close to?"

"I mean, like way, way, way, in the past. When we first got together, I was still getting messages from girls I knew, and she wanted to know who they were. I just didn't talk to them anymore."

"Was she a jealous person? Did she check your phone?"

"She had full access to my phone."

"Did she then?"

"She would use it for face-book. She would make a post for me or something."

"Would you do that on her phone?"

"No. She used it sometimes if her phone would mess up. She knew I couldn't spell."

"How long did the conversation last?"

"From about 4:15 a.m. to about 5:00, I guess."

"I'm a little confused. You talked about the selling the house to get something cheaper, and yet you were talking about how you didn't love her anymore."

"I wanted to talk about the house, because if we do separate we would have money to ourselves. She told me before, if we ever separate neither one of us can make if on our own."

"So you weren't talking about you guys downsizing somewhere? It was more like splitting everything?"

"Yeah, we could have some money left over and still be close to each other."

"So what other bills do you have?"

"Medical bills. Shanann had surgery on her back and we were still paying that off."

"When was that?"

"Sometime last year. Yeah, because her friend Christina came from Hawaii to help and it was during football season, so August or September? And the girls also had a lot of medical bills."

"What medication were they on?"

"They had inhalers, and CeCe had Singular, and something for acid reflux."

"What other big bills?"

"Credit card bills, but I am not sure how much we owed. She handled all of the finances. The one dumb thing I did was selling my four-wheeler for less than I owed on it."

"What about car payments?"

"Her car is paid for by Le-Vel."

"Any other big bills?"

"We filed for bankruptcy two years ago. We owed on furniture and stuff. The medical wasn't part of it, or the house."

"How would you classify your finances?"

"When the kids go back to school, it's pretty much check to check. I mean she had taken out a loan against my 401K to catch up on the house payment. We were almost three months behind."

"How did she feel about it?"

"She was stressed out about it."

"Do you have health insurance through your work?"

"Yeah, we do."

"How about life insurance?

"I've got one for Shanann, through work, and then a policy for each of the girls through work. Bella and CeCe have $20.000 each, and Shanann was $50,000 or $100,000."

"So how long was the talk that you had in the bed?"

"Until about 5:00 a.m."

"And she told you she was taking the kids to a friends, but she didn't mention who?"

"Yeah, I called her later and asked where she was, so I would know how the kids were doing."

"Okay, and you do what after you get out of bed?"

"I went downstairs, made a protein shake, and got my stuff ready for work."

"Where was the truck?"

"I usually park across the street. Someone was going through the cars and garages in our neighborhood, stealing things. I parked on the street so my neighbor's camera would see my truck. He told me where to park so the camera would catch it. I backed up to the garage. It was the weekend and I knew I had a lot of stuff so I wanted to make loading easier. I have two big containers in the back seat, so I put the stuff in there."

"How long did it take you to load your truck?"

"About fifteen minutes, maybe."

"How far into the garage were you?"

"About ¾ of the way."

"How often do you take your tools out?"

"I usually do it on Friday."

"Is that normal, that you would take everything out, and then load it back up the next week?"

"Yeah, that's a normal thing for me."

"When you pulled out, you shut the garage door?"

"Yeah." Chris proceeded to explain how the motion sensor works in the house, and the only thing that seemed odd was that the garage door indicated it wasn't shut when he left in the morning. The basement door indicated that it was opened about the same time. He explained that the basement door is off the garage. It doesn't have an alarm but it does have a sensor. It definitely wasn't open when he left. Tammy asked Chris about the route he takes to work and he gave her a detailed account.

"Do you have a GPS on your truck?"

"Yeah, but it isn't a regular one. It shows if I'm speeding."

"So which well did you go to first? Was anyone else there?"

"They showed up later."

"You were by yourself out there?"

"Yeah, there was a trouble area and I wanted to address it early."

"So you're at Cervi 319 at 6:45. What time do other people show up?"

"Probably between 7:15 and 7:30."

"Did they see you? Did you have a conversation?"

"Yeah."

"Why were they not there when you were?"

"They went to the office first. I usually go to the office first, but I knew there was a leak there and I wanted to get right on it. I didn't want a health or environmental problem."

"Did you pick up anyone on the way, or stop at a convenience store or gas station?"

"No."

"Besides the co-workers you already told us about, did anyone else see you?"

"No."

"As far as your work truck goes, are you allowed to let anyone ride in it?"

"The kids have played in the truck a few times."

"How about Shanann? Has she ever been in your truck before?"

"Not to work, but she's been in it a few times. We aren't allowed to take civilians around, but other Anadarko employees can ride with me."

"So when you arrived at the house, you opened the garage door and looked around for Shanann and the girls. Tell me what you thought looked odd about the situation."

"It was odd that the car was there with the car seats. Her purse, wallet, and the phone still being there was a big thing for me."

"It sounds like she was pretty attached to her phone."

"Yeah, everybody knows she is really attached to her phone. And the kid's medicine, that was weird."

"What about Shanann? Does she take any meds?"

"She takes Imitrex for migraines and that was not in her purse."

"Did you go through her luggage yet, looking for clues?"

"I haven't gone through it yet."

"You said the kids bedding was pulled back."

"The beds weren't made."

"Is that normal?" Tammy asked.

"Pretty normal."

"And your bed, what did that look like?"

"The sheets were off. When she gets home from a flight or a trip, she washes the sheets the next day."

"Are those sheets were in a pile where she was going to wash them?"   "I think I washed everything," Chris responded.

"Oh, did you put them away in the closet?'

"They should be in a pile on the floor or something."

"So, did you wash the sheets that were on the bed, or just put on new sheets?"

"I washed the sheets that were on the bed. They should still be in the room."

"In a clean pile?"

"I put clean sheets from the closet on the bed."

"So the beds are made now?"

"Oh yeah, definitely."

"So when you slept there Monday, you put new sheets on the bed because it was already stripped?"

"Yeah."

"Anything else that was odd? You said there were some things missing from the kid's room."

"Their 'binkies'."

"What do you think about that?"

"I mean that's what kids always take with them. The kids always take them.
Yeah, CeCe wants her Yankees blanket and Bella wants her blanket, especially if she feels like…" Chris paused in the middle of his sentence. "We tell her to leave it at the house, because she is getting old enough." Chris's voice softened each time he spoke about his girls.

"Even if you are going to the store or running errands, do they take them?"

"Bella will. CeCe takes the Yankees blanket, and the little dog that makes sounds."

"And you said that was gone, right?"

"Yeah, Bella's cat is still there."

"Was she as attached to her cat as CeCe was to her dog?"

"Not as much," Chris answered.

"Anything else missing, anything weird?"

Chris shook his head no.

"What about the pajamas you put them in? The nightgowns?" Tammy continued.   "I didn't see those. I mean there is dirty laundry from the kids. There were nightgowns in there, but not the ones I described to you."

"Obviously you have had a lot of time to clear your thoughts, and you've been talking to me. What are you thinking about now?"

"The first thing I thought was that she was at a friend's house, decompressing. But now, after yesterday and today, I feel like she's not safe, like she's in trouble or somebody hurt her and the kids. We can't find them. We don't know where they are."

"So if I ask you on the polygraph test if you caused Shanann's disappearance can you pass that? What do you think I mean by that?"

"If you asked me that, I feel like you're asking me if I had anything to do with it myself, or did I help somebody do it, and I had no part in that."

"I know it's awful to think about, but I need to know that you understand what I'm talking about. What are ways to make someone disappear?"

"I mean, like, what I've seen in the movies, or what you read about. Like hire somebody."

"Like a hitman?" Tammy offered.

"Yeah, I mean I'm just being honest," Chris assured her.

"That's what I want. I want you to go through all of these scenarios in your head because I want you to know what I'm talking about when I ask you if you physically caused her disappearance."

Chris continued, "Like hire somebody, or if you have someone you know who might do it." He laughed nervously at the conversation. "I mean it's a hard question to answer. I had nothing to do with the disappearance so I don't even want to think about..." Chris drifted off before he continued speaking. "Like, are you are asking me how I would do it?"

"No, anyone. How would anyone cause someone else to disappear?"

"I mean you would..."

"I mean you could cause someone's disappearance by murdering them. Do you agree with that?" Tammy asked.

"Yes."

"So what physical way could you cause someone's disappearance, though murder? You could stab someone, right?" Tammy continued.

"Stab someone, shoot someone, or hit them with a blunt object. I mean, use a weapon like a gun or knife." Chris took a long pause. "You could smother someone."

"You could strangle someone," Tammy offered.

"Yeah, all that kind of stuff. It's hard to even think about that stuff right now," Chris responded. The topic was clearly not one he wanted to discuss.

"You could strangle someone. You could drown someone." Tammy went on.

"Yeah."

"You could shock someone to death or burn someone alive. What other ways can you think of?" Tammy asked.

"As far as, like, lure them into a trap."

"What do you mean?"

"Like have someone waiting around the corner."

"You could kidnap them and lock them up in a basement somewhere. You know what I mean, they could still be alive," Tammy added.

"You could take them somewhere and torture them, and let them sit there without food or water," Chris suggested.

"You could kidnap them, and leave them somewhere where they aren't being tortured, where they can't get out. They disappear because they are being held and they can't be seen by society or the public. Does that make sense?" Tammy asked.

"Yeah."

"What other ways could you make someone disappear?"

"Poison," Chris suggested.

"Okay," Tammy responded. Chris was still. The silence in the room hovered over Chris and Tammy. The only sound came from the relentless clock, tick, tick, tick.

Tammy finally broke the deafening silence, "Sorry, this is…"

"I know! You could beat someone I guess, to the point where they are unconscious and they're in a coma," Chris continued the unusual speculative conversation.

"So if I ask you that question on the test Chris, are you going to have any issue with that, about physically causing their disappearance?"

"I can definitely pass that," Chris assured her.

"I mean you could murder them, you could kidnap them, you could take them to another country, you know, bury them in your back yard," Tammy continued. "You could do a million things, at first, trying to conceal them, right? So no one can find them. At this point she's gone and the girls are gone. We don't know where they are. So we are assuming the worst but hoping for the best, you know what I mean? You are kind of in that spot too. If I asked you the question, if you physically caused her disappearance? I say physically caused, because everyone has guilt, right? And I don't want you to feel like 'I told her that, I didn't want to be with her anymore so I probably caused her disappearance, and she took off with the girls because of what I told her'."

"That's why I feel like a jackass right now."

"So when I ask you the question, I'm not asking you about guilt. I'm not asking if you made her feel so horrible she ended up leaving. I'm asking if you are the one that physically caused her to disappear, either by murder, kidnapping, or any of those other scenarios that we went through. Okay?"

"Do you want me to list all of those?"

"No, no. You can just say no. So, do you have any issues with that or have any questions about what I would mean when I ask you that?"

"No. I just, going through all of those, that's a lot to think about. Trying to think about..." Chris drifted off in thought.

"It's a lot, but it's very simple. You didn't have anything to do with her physical disappearance. Maybe you pissed her off to the point that she ended up taking off with the kids, or maybe she became suicidal and killed herself, and we just haven't found her yet."

"Like, I feel emotionally responsible, but I didn't actually hurt her."

"Right, I want to ask you about physically causing her disappearance, that you were the one. I'm going to ask you about Shanann. I think we can all assume that wherever she is the little girls are with her. So I'm just going to ask you about Shanann," Tammy explained.

"Okay."

"The next question I'm going to ask you. Are you lying about the last time you saw her?"

"No," Chris stated immediately.

"Describe the last time you saw her."

"The last time I saw her, she was in bed after I talked to her. She was just physically lying in bed."

"Was she still crying? Was she saying anything?"

"She had just told me she was going to go to a friend's house with the kids and she would be back later. That was the last time I saw her."

"So describe what she looked like. Was she on her back, on her side?"

"On her side. On her right side."

"Could you see her face?"

"Yes."

"Describe what she looked like."

"She had mascara running down her face. She hadn't taken her makeup off before she went to bed that night."

"To your knowledge, that's the last time you would have seen her?"

"That's the last time I saw her, and the last time I saw the kids was in the monitor."

"We have to talk about worst-case scenarios. If for some reason you murdered her that would not be the last time you saw her. Do you agree with that?"

"I agree with that."

"The last question I want to ask you is if you know where Shanann is now."

"I do not."

"Obviously you have talked to the police. You are helping with the missing person's investigation. So this would be more like Shanann called you and asked you not to say where she is. Maybe she just needed to get away, and wanted to keep her location on the down-low, or whatever. Maybe, if you helped someone murder her, dumped her body somewhere, you would know where that site was. If the last time you saw her was in the bed, with make up running down her face, then you wouldn't know where she is. Do all of the questions make sense to you?"

"Yes."

"What would your answers be to all of those questions?"

"I had nothing to do with what's going on right now. I did not physically harm her. Last time I saw her was in bed, lying on her side, with mascara on her face, after we had a conversation and I do not know where she is."

"Who do you think would have hurt Shanann and the girls?"

"We have been over every option, like people we know."

"Even if it sounds crazy, what is your most pressing thought about what could have happened?"

"Someone I don't know anything about, has Shanann and the kids, and they aren't safe right now. They have been physically hurt."

"We are going to have to expect the worse and hope for the best. If we do find your wife and your two girls murdered, what do you think should happen to that person?"

"Life in prison, or the death penalty. Those are the only two things you really can do."

"Do you know anything you haven't told detectives that you want to share with us today?" Tammy asked.

"No, we are trying to reach out to friends and family. We have nothing else that might let us know who could have her, or where she could be."

"We are going to take a bathroom break, and then I am going to tell you more about how the polygraph works. You already know the kinds of questions I am going to be asking."

Chris and Tammy left the room, left the silence. When Chris returned from using the bathroom, he neatly placed his wallet and phone back on the small table. He sighed deeply and stretched his shoulders. They were stiff from the uncomfortable chair he had spent the last few hours sitting in. Thoughts of different ways to commit murder, life in prison, the death penalty, all lingered in the room like a bad smell. Chris subtly nodded his head back and forth a few times, as if he could not believe situation he found himself in. He stared blankly at the wall in front of him and then at the floor. He gently chewed on his lip. He leaned way back in his chair, stretching the tension that surrounded him tightly like a rubber band. Tammy came back in the room carrying a soda. She offered Chris one.

"No thanks, I haven't had one of those in years."

"Well don't start now, Tammy joked. Do you have any bad habits?"

"I used to. Soda was my go-to for a while."

"Let's go over the questions I am going to ask. Is that cool with you? Just so you'll know the wording of all the questions and there are no surprises," Tammy stated.

"Am I allowed to breath and, um?"

"Yes, you are obviously still a person and there are functions that you need to stay alive. We just don't want you to move a bunch. I'll explain that to you. And it's for very short periods of time. I have no doubt, being the healthy guy that you are, you'll have no problem with that, okay?"

"Okay."

"You will know every question. The first question will be regarding Shanann's disappearance. Do you intend to answer all of the questions truthfully?"

"Yes."

"And you are only going to get to answer yes or no to these questions, okay?"

"Oh, alright."

"This is the first relevant question I am going to ask. Did you cause Shanann's disappearance?"

"No."

"Are you lying about the last time you saw Shanann? And then, do you know where Shanann is now? Those are three we discussed before. You are going to be taking a direct-to-lie polygraph, so there will be questions on the test where I want you to lie. I want to see what your body looks like when you are telling a lie. I know it seems kind of weird, but you're going to know which questions these are, and they are going to be easy to answer. The first one. Before 2018 did you ever lose your temper with someone you cared about? We have all lost our temper. Don't tell me, but I want you to have the moment in your mind, when you lost your temper with someone you cared about."

"Okay."

"Whether it was with Shanann, your parents, your children, with anyone."

"Do you want me to say no to that one?" Chris asked.

"Yes, because we have all lost our temper. All of the questions you should lie about will start, before 2018. That is the clue that this is one of those questions you are expected to lie to, on the test. The next one. Before 2018 did you ever say anything out of anger to a loved one? Take a moment and think of a time when that occurred. We have all done it. Do you have something in your head?"

"Yeah."

"I want you to think of that when you answer the question on the test. The last one. Before 2018 have you ever wanted to hurt someone to get even with them? Not that you actually hurt them, but maybe they pissed you off so bad, you were, like, 'I wish I could punch that guy in the face right now'. Think about a time when that occurred. The next questions are known truth questions.

They will be really easy to answer. Is your first name Christopher? Were you born in 1985? Are you now in the state of Colorado? Are you now sitting down? Are the lights on in this room? Do you understand that I will only ask you the questions we have discussed? That's the last question. Those are the only questions you will hear come out of my mouth. Tammy went through the questions one more time with Chris, as he answered all of the questions with a yes or no answer. Any of those questions give you heartburn, or make you uneasy?

"My heart is, like," Chris paused. "I'm nervous."

"And this isn't a process where you shouldn't be nervous. That is to be expected. Did you do any research on polygraphs?"

"No, I just know what I have seen on TV. The lines move up and down. Does it go off of your heart beat, or?"

"I'll explain the components when I put them on you."

"I mean, when I came in here my heart was going a million miles a minute, and that hasn't stopped."

"The second I put all of the components on, you it will feel like, 'oh shit this just got real'," Tammy explained. "Everyone has that moment when the equipment is attached. Have you ever been pulled over before?"

"Yes, I had a mustang."

"Oh, I'll bet you were pulled over a lot," Tammy teased. "So I am going to explain a polygraph in a way that makes sense to me. I like to ask people about a time when they were pulled over, and how they felt at that time. That moment when you see the lights, or know the police are going to pull you over. I ask people to describe how they felt at that moment. Most people have their heart beating out of their chest. They start hyperventilating. Some people get mad, some get sad. All of the things that are happening to your body at the time are regulated by your automatic nervous system. Whenever your brain senses that you are in a stressful situation it automatically kicks in, and there are automatic changes to your body. Your body thinks it needs to help keep you alive. Have you heard of fight or flight before? Say you're walking in the woods and you hear a bear growl. If you fight the bear, you go free, or you run away. At that point you can't really process what's happening. I am going to give you three options on how to keep you alive. Some people are, like, 'what the hell does that mean'? I'm sure from a very young age your father taught you it is wrong to lie, or steal. Would you agree to that?"

"Yeah."

"And there are consequences for lying, or stealing. So if I asked you a question and the answer is yes, but the word no, comes out of your mouth, your brain will automatically sense that you are in a threatening situation, because it knows there are consequences for lying. It doesn't really matter to your brain if you are grounded on a Friday night, or you are going to spend the rest of your life in prison. Your brain doesn't differentiate the severity of the consequences. It just goes 'holy cow' and your body reacts to the situation. Being pulled over by the police, facing a bear in the woods, or lying on a polygraph. All of these situations are going to cause the same kind of physical reaction. So I am going to be reading these signs in your body when you are answering questions. I do that by attaching these components to you. Based on the questions we discussed, I will see what your body looks like when you are telling the truth, and when you are telling a lie."

"I thought it was just based on my heart rate, which is beating like crazy."

"You are your own baseline. I don't compare you to anyone else. So if your heartbeat is really fast, that's your baseline."

Tammy proceeded to hook Chris up to the polygraph equipment. She had Chris put his hands together, and place them on his forward like he was diving, and then she had him lean forward. She wrapped a cord around Chris's waist, and one around his chest. She then placed a blood pressure cuff on his right calf. Chris was cooperative, but seemed nervous, slightly chewing on his bottom lip. She put a device on the finger-tips of Chris's right hand to monitor his sweat rate. She instructed him to leave his hand flat on the table."

"What is the mat for?" Chris asked, referring to the mat that Tammy placed under his feet.

"That is going to record all of your movement. If you move your little toe that will record it. It is very sensitive. Tammy went over a pre-test, indicating when she wanted him to lie. Chris continued to chew his lip lightly. She set her clipboard in front of Chris and asked him to look directly at it, not side to side. "You do need to remain completely still. No belching, or sneezing."

"Just breathing."

"Yes, breathing." They both laughed, easing the tension that was mounting in the room. "If I need to ask you to correct something during the test, say you're moving your little finger, please just fix it. Don't move around or apologize. During the test you cannot look at me. I will be staring at you, and I know it feels goofy having someone stare at you when you can't look back, but that is kind of the name of the game today."

"Okay."

"There is no talking during the test. The only time you speak, is when you say yes or no. Try not to move your head when you answer. Your whole body needs to be still. There is no air in your cuff right now, but I am going to over inflate the cuff and it will feel like your leg is going to fall off for a few seconds. I then let almost all of the air out and pump it up about half way. Please let me ask a question in its entirety before you answer it."

Tammy proceeded to set things up on her computer while Chris looked nervously around the room. He stretched his neck and looked up at the ticking clock. Tammy sat down and asked Chris to relax until she told him it was time to start the polygraph. "We are about to begin, please remain still."

Chris sat like a statue, looking straight ahead. The only sound in the room was the now familiar, tick, tick, tick, from the clock. Tammy asked Chris a series of questions regarding numbers he had written on a page. Chris had been instructed to answer no to every question, even if the answer was yes, so Tammy could establish a baseline and see Chris's physical condition when he was purposefully lying. Chris answered no to every question per her instructions. His answers were heavy as if he couldn't catch his breath. The tick, tick, tick, now unbearably loud, echoed through the room between each long pause, each question and answer. Chris sat silently, not moving a muscle.

"This portion of the test is complete. Please remain still while I take the instrument out of operation."

Once allowed to move, Chris shook off the moment.

"How do you feel? You did great. You remembered to lie and everything."

"That was, ah," Chris was a bit overcome by the experience.

"You are obviously, a very bad liar. Have people told you that before? On question three, when you purposefully lied, I had to turn down the machine because of the sensitively. It was going off the page. That is what I need to see, because it tells me you know it is wrong to tell a lie. Thank you for being a horrible liar. That just shows that when we are asking significant questions about your wife, if you lie, it will be amplified ten times. When asking questions we have to ask at least three times. The cool thing about this, right now there is only one person in this room who knows what the truth is, and in about five minutes there will be two of us. That's the coolest part, and then I can go share that with the others."

"Okay, ah, my heart is beating out of my chest," Chris declared.

"Yep, you are creating your own baseline so you're good."

Chris fidgeted in the chair and moved around uncomfortably.

"The clipboard you were looking at is gone, so focus on the back of the chair directly in front of you, but not so hard that you go cross eyed. Just look straight ahead. Do you remember the questions you are supposed to lie about?"

"Whenever a question begins with, before 2018, I need to lie."

"Right, and you are going to think about the lie that you will tell, like we practiced?"

"Yeah."

"Are you ready?"

"Do it!"

"The test is about to begin. Please remain still. Do you understand I will only ask you the questions we have discussed?"

"Yes."

There were long pauses between the questions, tick, tick, tick. It was difficult for Chris to determine which sound was louder, the clock, or the beating of his own heart.

"Regarding Shanann's disappearance, do you intend to answer all of the questions truthfully?"

"Yes."

"Is your first name Christopher?"

"Yes."

"Just breathe normally. Before 2018 did you ever lose your temper with someone you cared about?"

"No."

"Did you physically cause Shanann's disappearance?"

"No," Chris's answer was subdued.

"Were you born in 1985?"

"Yes."

"Before 2018 did you ever say anything out of anger to a loved one?"

"No," Chris lied per the instructions.

"Are you lying about the last time you saw Shanann?"

"No."

"Are you now in the state of Colorado?"

"Yes," Chris' answered quietly.

"Before 2018 did you ever want to hurt someone to get even with them?"

"No."

"Do you know where Shanann is now?"

"No."

"This portion of the test is complete," Tammy informed Chris that he could relax.   Tammy   sat back in her chair and leaned on her hand. "How do you feel?"

"Horrible, trying to look at something without anything there."

"The chair thing?" Tammy inquired.

"Yeah."

"I know, it gets kind of weird."

"I feel, ah, just trying to figure out how to stay still," Chris admitted.

"Do you have any issues with the questions? You know what I'm talking about when I asked about Shanann's disappearance?"

"Yeah, I'm there."

Chris took a small sip of water while Tammy teased him about wanting a soda now. He didn't share in her joke this time, as she prepared for the next section of the test. He repositioned himself, hand flat on the table, feet on the mat.

"I'm getting everything stable," Chris explained.

"All good like that?" Tammy asked.

"Yeah, I'm good." Chris stretched his neck back and forth while Tammy adjusted the instruments that were wrapped around his chest.

"During the last test you were breathing really hard, so please just try to take normal breaths, okay? We can't have deep breathes."

"Oh, no deep breath, sorry."

"Just breathe as normally as possible, okay?" Tammy said patiently.

"Yeah."

"Are you ready?" She asked.

"Yeah."

Tammy pumped up the blood pressure cuff and then released some of the air.

"The test is about to begin, please remain still," Tammy instructed.

Chris sat perfectly still, uncomfortably staring into the nothingness.

"Do you understand I will only ask you the questions we have discussed?"

"Yes," Chris answered quietly.

"Regarding Shanann's disappearance, do you intend to answer all of the questions truthfully?"

"Yes."

"Are you now in the state of Colorado?"

"Yes."

"Before 2018 have you ever wanted to hurt someone to get even with them?"

"No."

"Are you lying about the last time you saw Shanann?"

"No."

"Is your first name Christopher?"

"Yes."

"Before 2018 did you ever lose your temper with someone you cared about?"

"No."

"Do you know where Shanann is now?"

"No," Chris answered rapidly.

"Were you born in 1985?"

"Yes."

"Before 2018 did you ever say anything out of anger to a loved one?"

"No."

"Just breathe normally. Did you physically cause Shanann's disappearance?"

"No."

"The test is now complete. I would like to get one more chart, set of questions, but I really need your breathing to be normal. You were all over the place."

"Sometimes I feel like I'm not breathing enough, and then I don't want to breathe too hard."

"Yeah, I just need you to breathe as normally as possible and not fluctuate, okay."

"Sorry about that."

"I just want to do one more set instead of three more," Tammy explained.

"Yeah, I don't want that," Chris said as he took a big swig of water.

"Okay, let's go again." Tammy reset the blood pressure cuff. "Breathe normally. Regarding Shanann's disappearance, do you intend to answer all of the questions truthfully?"

"Yes."

"Were you born in 1985?"

"Yes."

"Before 2018 did you ever say anything out of anger to a loved one?"

"Yes, no," Chris quickly corrected his answer.

"Do you know where Shanann is now?"

"No."

"Are you now in the state of Colorado?"

"Yes."

"Before 2018 have you ever wanted to hurt someone because you were angry with them?"

"No."

"Did you physically cause Shanann's disappearance?"

"No."

"Is your first name Christopher?"

"Yes."

"Before 2018 did you ever lose your temper with someone you cared about?"

"No."

"Are you lying about the last time you saw Shanann?"

"No."

"The test is now complete. Please remain still while I take the instruments. All right, how did you feel? The same through all of it?" Tammy proceeded to unhook Chris from her instruments. He assisted her as she removed the cords from around his waist and chest.

"It's kind of hard to relax," Chris admitted how stressed out he was.

"I know. Let me get that," Tammy said, as she removed the cuff from his calf.

"I feel like my feet were sweating. I'm a hot person."

"I need to go grade this. Do you need to use the restroom?"

"I'm good right now."

Tammy collected her laptop. "I'll be right back," she informed Chris, as she left the room.

Chris reached for the Gatorade he had on the table. He opened it and took several large swigs. He bent his head down, looking at the floor, moving occasionally to take a swig of the blue Gatorade. The room was silent except for the relentless tick, tick, tick. The dread in the room was intensifying. Chris finished the Gatorade, picked up the water bottle, and drank the rest of his water. Chris sat up straight in his chair and stared blankly at the wall. The minutes dragged by, and he could think of nothing but being allowed to leave this room. He had spent hours with Tammy. He was tired of talking, tired of sitting, and he had never wanted to leave a room more than at this moment. He started rolling his head to release the built up tension in his neck. The waiting was agonizing, but not knowing what was coming next was worse. After a miserable thirty minutes passed, Tammy finally reentered the room.

"Are you okay?" she asked.

"Yeah."

"I just want to pack this stuff up, and then Graham is going to come in for a chat, okay. You need anything, crackers, water, or a soda?"

"No, I'm good. Is my dad out there?"

"You know, I bet Graham knows."

"Can I check my phone or should I just let it be?" Chris glanced at his phone sitting on the table.

"You can check, it's up to you."

"I'll bet Shanann's mom has called five or six times by now. Yeah, she also called the detective. Did she know you were coming in here today?"

"No," Chris responded.

"Who knew you were coming in today?"

"My friends Nick and Amanda, because I stayed with them last night, and my dad."

"What did your dad say about it?"

"He told me to just answer whatever questions, and just do what you ask." Chris found a picture of the girls on his phone and showed Tammy.

"Oh, they are adorable. They look bigger than I thought. I saw a picture of them on the news and they were much smaller. Chris scrolled his phone and mentioned that he wasn't getting service in the room."

"Are you still getting messages from work?"

"No, everybody is checked out now."

Tammy and Chris continued to chat about his work. Chris was pretty talkative about his fellow employees, explaining that they had all been very supportive. Tammy was busy wrapping up all of her equipment.

"I'm going to run this stuff out real quick," she told him.

"Okay."

All of the equipment was out of the room and Chris sat alone once more with his thoughts and his fears. He leaned over in the chair again, and stared at the floor silently for a few minutes. Chris suddenly took out his phone and pulled up a video of his family. The sound of Shanann's voice filled the empty room as she spoke to her daughters, as their little voices responded with joy and excitement. Chris listened to his own voice as he talked to his baby girls. His entire family was alive and well on the four inch screen. He played the video, over, and over again. A knock on the door fractured the moment, and his family fell away into the void of a black screen.

Chapter 8

The experience with Speaks With Stars on the cliff had been exhilarating. In the moment, Shanann believed that everything was right with the world. Bella was fine and she would be with her soon. But she was back in her house now, and the feelings of ease were overtaken by worry and anxiety. Shanann walked slowly through her home. All of her things were here, everything she had so carefully saved for and picked out. She tried to connect with the past, with her life in this place, but she couldn't remember why all of these things had been so important to her. Her life here was fading. She only wanted her children. She wanted to see where her marriage stood. If Chris didn't love her anymore, she would figure it out. Even though it would be almost impossible with three kids, she was strong and creative and she would make it work somehow! She couldn't walk around confused for one more second. This time, it was very clear where she should be. Shanann walked outside. He was sitting there waiting for her. She walked over, picked up a stick and stoked the fire. Speaks With Stars took a deep draw from his pipe and then offered it to Shanann.

"No, I want to be clear now. I need to figure out what happened so I know where to look for Bella."

"It sounds like you have reached a point of resolve," he responded.

"Yes, it is time to find my girl." Shanann sat quietly for several moments, as if her mind was informing itself, leading her to answers, to clarity, to Bella. "My husband is having an affair," Shanann said with sadness, but determination. "He is my love story. I thought I was his.

144

I know I'm not the perfect wife. I'm an Italian woman. We love fully, we are demanding, and we are aggressive. But we always try to make the most of life and we are amazing cooks," Shanann said with a little laugh. "Chris and I are opposites. He is calm and passive. At first, I thought it was a great fit. Opposites attract, you know. He seemed to want me to be the director. He is definitely more comfortable being directed. Sometimes I got tired of making all of the decisions, but he was just as set in his ways as I was in mine and we settled. Our relationship became regimented." Shanann sat quietly in deep thought before she continued, "There is no way to shake his systematic way of doing things, to penetrate it, get to something deeper. He responds in the right way, always. It's almost like he's reading a script, and deviating in any way is unthinkable. How do you complain about a person who is doing everything you ask? He doesn't have any emotional cracks. He never loses his temper. We never argue about anything important. There is no place to push in and break open his persona. Do you know how frustrating that is for an emotional, Italian woman?"

Speaks With Stars smiled. Yes, he knew what a strong woman was like. "It must have been exhausting for him, never taking off that mask."

Shanann thought for a moment. "I guess it is. I know it's exhausting for me, trying to break into his emotional vault. At some point I stopped trying so hard. I relented and just enjoyed the fact that he seemed pliable. We established a way of doing things, but as the girls started getting older, growing their own personalities, it seemed to put more pressure on him. He isn't comfortable drifting in and out of our established patterns. We have great kids, but they are still kids. They get cranky and unreasonable, and CeCe is a whirlwind of activity. I can see the frustration in his eyes. He gets close to the edge, but for some reason he can't stray from the idea of what a good dad is supposed to look like, behave like. I, on the other hand, have very strong opinions and they come out, a lot, in Italian fashion, loudly and intensely. I wish he felt more comfortable. This parenting stuff isn't going to get easier. I thought we were okay. Apparently we aren't! And now there is another woman. If he loves her..." Shanann drifted off and let out a deep sigh. She was clearly perplexed and distraught at the thought of Chris with someone else. "How does everything change so drastically in five weeks? He acted like everything was just fine. Is it possible he has been pretending our entire marriage?" Shanann asked, her voice shaking with feelings of deep hurt and betrayal.

"Pretending?" Speaks With Stars repeated the word with a quizzical look on his face.

"You know, acting," Shanann stated.

Speaks With Stars shook his head. He wasn't familiar with the word.

Shanann tried to explain, "When someone is false. When they act a certain way, but it isn't really how they feel. They are pretending, see?"

"Like, Inktomi, the spider-trickster," Speaks With Stars said with acknowledgment.

"I guess so. If someone is pretending, I guess they are trying to trick you in some way, or, maybe trick themselves?" Shanann pondered.

"Inktomi is complicated, good and bad. He is cunning and sly. In the stories of our people, the spider-trickster often outsmarts himself, and his endeavors may not end well."

Shanann paused to reflect on the words of Speaks With Stars.

"How about the family of your husband?" Speaks With Stars, asked.

"His dad is his hero. Chris and Ronnie are a lot alike. They rarely express their feelings, but they have a solid bond. His mom, well, it wasn't good from the very beginning. His parents didn't even come to our wedding. I never met his mother's expectations. She criticizes everything about me, but in a passive way. She hates that Chris bought me an expensive engagement ring. I can understand that she thought it cost too much, but I never understood why she couldn't let go of the resentment. It has been years now. It is almost like she keeps it in her quiver until she needs it. Her verbal arrows are subtle, but effective, and they never miss. It hurts him deeply and sometimes I feel like I have to protect him. It feels like a part of Chris is locked away, and it is too risky for him to come out," Shanann said, letting out a deep sigh. "We did have really good times with his family, but there is some kind of a disconnect I don't fully understand. When I am around my family I feel safe speaking my mind. We don't always agree, that's for sure, but there aren't murky, anxiety filled spaces. We know where we stand and we move our arms a lot," Shanann said with a twinkle in her eye.

Speaks With Stars thought about what his young friend was saying, pondering over his own experiences. "When the white men came, my people were torn from the old ways. Without considering the consequences, our young men they did things that ended up being bad for the tribe. The white man did not understand the needs of the young men and their desire to prove themselves as warriors. Some of them were so enraged by what was happening to our people, and the horrors inflicted upon us, they buried themselves deeply and allowed a violent aspect of their personality to emerge. They felt betrayed, and could only see the hateful reality that was exploding our world. The warriors fought out of rage and self-preservation. These were the most dangerous of our young men, and the white leaders used their extreme actions as a projection of who my people were. The leaders told the white people that they needed to be afraid. And when the people looked into the soft brown eyes of a small native child, they only saw someone who wanted to grow tall and kill them. The trick worked. Fear grew, and the white people lost sight of what was real. They lost themselves in a spider's web of misunderstanding, and the lie became their truth. The voices of my people, the ones who wanted to get along and live in peace, were drowned out. We did not stand a chance against the lie. We could not fight such hatred. The only solace we had, was with the mother. We were always connected to her. When someone was lost or confused, they could find themselves in the songs of the running water; in the breeze speaking through the trees; in the strength of the rocks. The earth responds to us, she teaches us. When the people were angry, when they felt desperate, they would come to the mother and feel her bond. She does not judge. The mother is always with us." Speaks With Stars took a deep breath, "Even then we were herded away from the lush land the mother had given us, and forced onto the barren plains, we were still grateful to her. We knew the land was all that would remain. The trinkets, and land titles, and ownership would all fade one day and the land would renew itself, despite the people who tried to use her up. And that would be the ultimate trick." Speaks With Stars smiled.

Shanann was deep in thought. She felt honored that Speak With Stars shared his experiences with her. She understood how it felt to be isolated and disconnected at times. Chris, however, could drift off like he was in a completely different world. It wasn't like someone losing focus, or not paying attention. Shanann tried to articulate her thoughts, "I know Chris doesn't always feel connected. It is hard for him to express his emotions. Maybe that's why he tries so hard to be the best version of himself."

"When a person doesn't express their emotions, when they swallow them instead of letting them out, they can build up emotional residue. Everyone does this to a certain degree. Pent up emotions come out in anger and in other ways. It is good to get them out. If someone builds up emotional residue for an entire lifetime, the release can be toxic, out of control," Speaks With Stars offered.

Shanann thought for a moment. That made perfect sense to her. "I think that is true. I always feel a release after I let off some steam, or have a good cry. It must feel terrible to not have an emotional release valve."

Speaks With Stars nodded, and spoke gently, "All things require a degree of balance." He took a long draw from his pipe.

Shanann collected her thoughts, trying to pull the scattered memories into a coherent timeline. "I remember his mom and I had a falling out. When I get back, I need to fix things with her." Shanann's gaze was drifting and the air was cooling down. Storm clouds were rolling in. She felt a shiver go down her spine and she was suddenly very cold.

"When you get back?" Speaks With Stars asked.

"Yes. I can't stay in this dream forever. Maybe I'm in a coma, weird!" Shanann's voice drifted off. She stood up suddenly without saying a word and entered her front door.

Chapter 9

Tammy and Graham entered the room and sat opposite one another, with Chris at the end of the small rectangular table.

"So I brought Graham in here, because we want to talk to you about the results, okay?"

"Okay."

Graham, in a long sleeve blue shirt, looking every bit like a serious FBI detective, put a notebook on the table, sat back, and looked directly at Chris. He was not smiling.

"It was really clear that you were not honest when you answered the questions. I think you already know that. You did not pass the polygraph test," Tammy informed.

"Okay," Chris answered quietly.

"So now, we need to talk about what actually happened. I feel like you are probably ready to do that," Tammy went on.

Chris immediately stated his claim, "I didn't lie to you on that polygraph, I promise."

Graham responded, "Chris. Chris, don't! Just stop for a minute. Take a deep breath. I want you to take a deep breath right now." Graham inhaled deeply, encouraging Chris to do the same.

Tammy spoke calmly, "There is a reason you feel sick to your stomach. When people hold stuff inside it makes them physically ill. And I can tell from your face, I can tell from the second you walked in, that you were wanting to just come clean and be done with this," Tammy continued. "And I appreciate that because you knew sitting down in that chair, that you weren't going to pass today, and you knew I was going to find out because I told you that, and you continued to stay, knowing that at the end you would be able to just get all of this off of your chest. We aren't here to play games. We don't want to do any of that. We just want to know what happened. Can you start from the beginning and tell us what happened?"

"Everything I told you, ah, I did not lie on the polygraph. I don't know how much I can tell you right now. I did not..."

Tammy interrupted. "That's not even an option right now because you did not pass the polygraph. I know you were being deceptive, so that is not the issue right now. The issue right now is what happened to Shanann, Bella, and Celeste. That's the issue right now."

"Okay," Chris responded, reluctantly.

"So let's talk about that. I know you want to tell us. I can see it in your face. Holding this lie, is going to do nothing for you," Tammy said, prodding Chris to face the facts.

"I know that. I'm not trying to cover things up," Chris stated.

Tammy responded, "But you are, kind of, and it's normal for people to do that. People who make a mistake initially, are going to deny it. That's normal, I would expect that. It's like asking your kid if they wrote on the wall, and they say no. And you can see that they have marker on their hands. It is a natural reaction to lie about something like that, and then eventually tell the truth. This is your eventually telling the truth time. This is where the rubber meets the road Chris. Don't let this continue any longer, please."

"I'm not trying to make anything continue. I want them back home."

"But you know they aren't coming back. You know that," Tammy stated.

"I don't know. In the back of my head, I hope they come back home," Chris stated.

Tammy repeated herself, "But you know they aren't."

"I hope they come back home. I don't know they're not coming back home."

Graham joined the conversation. "Chris, I'm confused. And here's what I'm confused about. I told you that we've done some work overnight. We had a lot of leads, and we know a lot more than we did. This is why we're confused. You're this great guy. I'm not just telling you that, okay. I'm telling you that, because everyone tells us that. We can't find anyone to say anything bad about you. Chris is a great guy. He's a good man. We're confused as to why you aren't taking care of your beautiful children."

"Why I'm not taking care of them right now?"

"Right now. Where are they?" Graham asked emphatically.

"I don't know," Chris answered, exasperated. I want them back. I want everybody back. That is the God's honest truth."

Both detectives stared at him intently. The sound of the clock seemed louder as if it was waiting for an answer, as well.

Graham breathed deeply without breaking his piercing gaze at Chris. He started again, "So, let's keep talking about your family, okay? We just can't figure out, well, there are two Chris's. We talked about that last night. We just can't figure it out."

"Yes."

"We just can't figure it out. There's this Chris, who surprises me, and warms my heart, because you are the kind of man who can pack a bag for his girls. You know what to put in the bag, and you know what to put in it as a backup in case they have an accident. You know the clothes to put in there. You know what they had for breakfast, and snack, and dinner, and the nighttime snack. You can tell me the book you read to your daughters. I know you love them and you're not faking it. It's real. There are a lot of guys who come in here and try to tell me that, and I know they are lying. They can't answer the questions you can answer. But you are here today, lying about something else, so we need to talk about that, okay," Graham continued in his attempt to appeal to Chris.

Chris blurted out, "I cheated on her."

"I know. And I know she's very good," Graham responded to Chris's admission.

"I'm not proud of it. I didn't think that could happen, that I would ever do it, but I did." Chris let out a sigh as if a heavy weight was lifted from him.

"I know, keep going," Graham encouraged.

"Shanann accused me of it. I denied it. I feel horrible for it. She is pregnant and, ah, I didn't hurt her. I cheated on her. I hurt her emotionally. I feel absolutely horrible. That's what I've been holding back. I didn't go to the Rockies game. I was with her. I went to dinner with her," Chris confided.

Graham is calm, and reassuring, as he listens to Chris, "Keep going."

"The five weeks I spent alone, I was with her most of the time."

"You're doing a good job. This is the Chris that I knew would come out. This is the Chris that tells the truth, because you are a truth teller. Who is 'her'? Graham asked.

"I don't want to get her involved in this. I don't want to ruin her life. I don't want her involved in this," Chris answered emotionally.

Graham responded, "Okay, I knew you would say you didn't want to get her involved."

"She's a wonderful person. She knew I was married, yes, and that we were going through issues. And I told her that at the end, we were going to be separated, once I figured out what that was, ah, I didn't know what that was going to be. I had no idea. I saw her, and she took my breath away, and I never thought in a million years that could happen. I know you think I'm a bigger guy, but it was, like, I never felt that way about anybody, any time," Chris spilled the words into the room as his thoughts drifted off. *Nikki is unlike anyone I've ever met.* He thought about the places they had gone, and how much fun they had together. *The car museum, the camping trip, the long conversations, the sex; she was like a roller coaster, and I couldn't get off.*

"Chris it's not your fault," Graham reasoned.

"No, no I'm just..." Chris was at a loss for words.

"Can we do this? I know you want to take care of her because you're the kind of guy who takes care of women. You are. You took care of your wife. You took care of your daughters. You are very good at taking care, and you want to take care of her. So can we make a deal? I don't think this girl did anything to hurt anybody, but I can't walk out of here wondering. So, we'll leave her out of it, and get back to your wife and daughters.

Okay, where are they?" Graham nudged Chris back to Shanann and the girls.

"I don't know. That was what I was holding back."

"Chris in the interview today, you weren't asked about infidelity."

"I was told I was holding back, from last night," Chris interrupted Graham, insisting that the secret he was holding was the affair he had been having.

"That's not how it works. You had reactions to every single question, not just the ones we talked about being important," Tammy reminded him.

"Like the ones you wanted me to lie about. Is that what you are talking about?"

"No, the questions about her disappearance, and knowing where she is, and when you last saw her."

"I was not lying about those things."

"Can I tell you what I think?" Graham asked.

"Yes."

"When you did the interview with Tammy and we hooked you up to the polygraph equipment, we already knew about Nikki. You're doing a very good job right now. You didn't have to tell us about her, but you did," Graham stated.

Chris admitted, "I couldn't hold it in any longer."

"I know. We could see it in your chest. We could see it in your eyes. Here's the challenge we have. We knew about Nikki, so we didn't need to ask about her on the polygraph. That's why we didn't ask, because we already knew. Now we are very worried about your daughters and your wife."

"I am too," Chris declared.

Graham continued, "Okay, I can tell you that based on all of the people Tammy and I have talked to; and all of the investigations that we have done; based on your cell phone, your wife's cell phone, Nikki's cell phone; based on talking with family members and friends, here's what we know. I'm not going to lie to you, here's what we know. Chris is a good man. That's what everyone said. I'm not just blowing smoke in your ear. Nobody can fake answers about packing their daughter's backpacks, nobody. It should have been the happiest time of your marriage. Shanann is making good money. You're making great money. You both have a job. You have beautiful kids. You have a beautiful house. You're in Colorado, clean air, good people. And on top of that you look pretty good now. You're pretty fit. This should have been a time in your marriage when you guys are happy, thriving and productive. I believe that Shanann is the reason none of that happened. I believe that she's a controlling person. Maybe she doesn't listen to you as much as she should. I think that she can do whatever she wants, and you can't. I think if you were to go to a restaurant, she would order whatever the hell she wants and as soon as you order a nice steak, she says 'whoa buddy'. A woman who lets her man do all of the backpack packing and all of the cooking," Graham continued luring Chris into a new line of conversation

"I didn't do all of the cooking, like, she cooks things here and there," Chris stated, half defending Shanann.

"I think that you are a good person, and she started on the path to leave the marriage. It's ironic that we're talking about you and Nikki. I think Shanann was the one who started on that path first. What do you think?" Graham continued to open up the storyline, to prod Chris into a different mode of conversation.

"I haven't thought about it."

"Another thing that is interesting. Even though she is that type of person that's controlling, doesn't listen, does what she wants, is walking away from her kids, here you are defending her because at your core you want to take care of the people you love. That's the reason why we want to give you an opportunity, today, to just help us find them. Will you do that for me?" Graham continued using his years of training, changing the narrative.

"I'll do whatever I can to help find them, to find out where they are."

"So when Tammy asked you, do you know where they are, or are you going to tell the truth about where they are, you failed miserably. Okay, why?"

"I'm a nervous person. With every question asked, it felt like I wasn't going to say the right thing."

"That's not how a polygraph works," Graham explained.

"I don't know how it reads. I know Tammy was talking about the autonomy of the process, but, I don't know where they are," Chris tried to explain.

"Chris, right now your dad's outside. He came across the country. You're lying to him." There was a long pause and the room fell deathly quiet. "You lied to everyone you talked to and they all bought it. Will you please help us find your babies?"

"I want to find them. I've told you over, and over, I want to find them." Chris's voice started to break.

"Okay, can we go back to that night?" Graham started over.

"Yeah."

"You know that we have texts, and we know there is an Alexa in your house, and you know those are trained to record distress. Do you know that we have the content of Nikki's text messages, and your text messages, and Shanann's text messages?"

"I didn't know about Nikki's texts, until right now."

"Tell us about that night again. Please tell us the truth this time."

"I told you the truth. I promise I've told you the truth. I woke up at 4:00 and I got dressed and got ready for work. At 4:15 Shanann and I talked about the house, about separation."

"You guys talk about Nikki?"

"She accused me of seeing someone else."

"You denied it?"

"She brought up the charge on the credit card, from the other night. It was for two people not just one," Chris admitted.

"And there were two of you, right? And at that time you weren't quite ready to say?"

"I couldn't say it. We already cried hard enough. I couldn't, I couldn't say that."

"What did you say?" Graham continued the rapid hardline of questioning.

"I told her I wanted a separation."

"Was it her idea to sell the house, or yours?"

"She initiated the conversation with the relator the week before."

"Why?"

"Because we were talking about the marital issues, and how we can't afford to live on our own, so she contacted the relator."

"Who did she contact?"

"Anne, our relator."

"If we asked Anne, would she say that it was your wife that contacted her?"

"Yes, she would. And then on Monday, I texted Anne to see what she could do."

"Prior to that, tell me about the pregnancy. Was that your idea or hers?"

"She was about 80%-20% against it, and I went over the pros and cons of it. After she got pregnant she told everybody that it was mainly my idea."

"Is that true? Did you want to get pregnant?"

"I was hoping for a boy. And after the fact, she said that I wanted the baby and she was 70%-30% against it, at that point. She told all of her friends that."

"Can you understand that some of this just doesn't make sense to us? How is it possible, that a woman and two kids are just completely gone off the face of the earth?"

"I promise you, I have nothing on my hands. I did nothing to the kids, or her, to make them vanish."

"So tell me what happened then? I believe that you did nothing with your hands, but what happened?"

"I left. It's on the video that I left. I was in my truck. I mean, I didn't load anything in my truck besides my tools, my container, my book bag, my water jug, my lunch box," Chris stated, sounding a bit frantic.

"Okay," Graham continued in a consoling tone. "But then what happened?"

"I drove out of the driveway."

"No, before you drove out of the driveway. What happened with your wife and your kids?"

"I didn't do anything like that. They were still in the house," Chris claimed.

"Where are they? Where did they go?" Graham's voice remained steady and consistent. He never raised his voice.

"I don't know, sir, I really don't know."

"Your wife's not the type of person to vanish."

"I know she's not."

"She had ten things on her schedule. That meant she was going to be there that day, the next day, with friends, with a doctor. She didn't leave because she wanted to. So what happened?" Graham continued to push.

"I didn't do anything to hurt her and the kids," Chris almost whispered the answer.

Tammy joined the conversation, "Was it an accident?"

Chris responded emphatically, "I didn't do anything."

"Was it an accident?" Tammy repeated the question.

"There was no accident. If there was an accident in the house, I wasn't there for it."

"It's a big deal if it's an accident, because we can work with that, Chris. Maybe that's what happened," Tammy added.

"I did not call it an accident. I didn't do anything to my wife and kids."

"Was it a misunderstanding?" Graham asked.

"We had a talk. There was a misunderstanding, because I didn't tell her about the affair. I didn't."

"Miscommunication, misunderstanding?" Graham continued.

"I probably should have told her right then. Honestly, I mean everything was out on the table anyway. I should have just told her right then, but I didn't. I just couldn't bring myself to do it."

"What was your plan? What were you going to do? How was the separation going to work?"

"Like, once we were separated, I would get my own place, and I was hoping for a 50/50 split with the kids."

"What about Nikki?" Graham asked.

"Take it slow, and see if anything developed when I had my own place."

Tammy stepped in again, "I find it hard hearing you talk about having this emotional conversation with Shanann, and you're bawling, and crying together, and you have not shed one tear in the two days that you've been here. Not one. Help me understand that, because I don't get it." Tammy positioned a photo lying on the table so that Chris could see it. "These are your baby girls and you have not shed one tear over them not being around. Chris, I lose my four year old in the store for ten seconds and I start to panic. Panic! I have not seen any of that from you, at all! Help me understand that."

"I love those girls. I would never do anything. Just because I haven't shed a tear."

"Yeah, that's weird, isn't that weird?" Tammy asked.

Chris became very emotional, "Don't look at it like I don't love my kids."

"Well then tell me. Explain it to me. You're crying with your wife, because you're telling her that you're leaving her, but you don't cry about your two little baby girls?"

"I am hoping they are still around. I am hoping they are still somewhere alive."

"You don't have them right now. You aren't reading them bedtime stories. You aren't giving them snacks. You aren't giving them their medicine, or waking up with them in the morning."

"I know that."

"So, that should cause you pain," Tammy pointed out.

"It does cause me pain."

"I don't see that. I don't see that. I want to see the Chris that cares. I want to see the Chris that feels bad about what he did, and wants to get this off his chest, and wants to be done with this. Let us find your little girls so they aren't out there in the middle of a field, or somewhere. Don't do that."

Chris's voice was filled with deep sorrow, "I love those girls."

"Then show us that. Show us that Chris," Tammy implored.

"I'm showing you the Chris that cares about the girls and his wife. Just because I haven't shed a tear doesn't mean the love isn't there for them."

"It's weird," Tammy responded.

"I understand that. I totally see where you are coming from. Trust me, just because..." Chris didn't finish his statement.

"People can be pushed to the point that they do something they regret. It happens every single day. But part of what makes you a man, is the guy that admits this is really fucked up. 'This is what I did and I'm going pay for what I did. I'm going to tell you what I did, and I'm going to be honest about it'," Tammy stated.

Graham jumped into the conversation, "We can keep talking to you about it, but once we find these girls, and your wife, no matter how we find them, no matter what condition they are in, you can tell us it isn't as bad as it looks. And you can say, 'let me tell you what happened'."

"Chris, did Shanann do something to them?" Tammy asked.

"No."

She continued, "I'm serious."

"I have no clue," Chris responded.

"You would have known, because they didn't leave the house. Did Shanann do something to them, and then you felt like you had to do something to Shanann?"

Chris shook his hands in frustration. "They were at the house when I left. They were there."

"They weren't there. They didn't leave. They vanished. The only way they could have left was in your truck," Tammy stated.

"No way, because I didn't just throw them in my truck."

"You know your truck has GPS, right?" Tammy asked.

"Yeah."

"You know that thing pings every ten seconds? So we will know exactly where you went?"

"And your company's giving that to us," Graham added.

"I know," Chris said quietly.

Graham continued, "Are we asking the right questions Chris?"

"You're asking all the questions."

"What are we not asking you? What are we doing wrong?"

"You aren't doing anything wrong," Chris answered.

"Did Shanann do something?" Tammy asked again.

"She didn't do anything to these kids. We both loved them will all of our hearts. There is no way."

"It could have been an accident. Something happened in that house that you know about. You failed the polygraph test. This is not about you leaving, and your wife vanishing, and you didn't know anything about it. That is not what you were asked. We know that something happened to all three of them, but I want to know if something happened to these baby girls first, and you had to take into your own hands, and deal with it," Tammy explained.

"You did the cleanup," Graham suggested.

"Chris, you have to tell us. Something happened to these baby girls." Tammy pointed to the photo on the table, "Look at them."

"I know. I was watching them on my phone for ten minutes."

"We have no doubt that you love girls with all your heart, no doubt. We all make mistakes. It's what we do with those mistakes, that make us who we are," Tammy stated.

"Chris you seem to be thinking about it right now. What are you thinking about?" Graham asked.

"I feel like you cleaned up for her. I feel like that's the type of guy that you are." Tammy pointed to the photo again. "Which daughter has the breathing problem?"

"Well they both use inhalers." Chris pointed to CeCe, and explained her medical condition.

"Did she have problems breathing?" Tammy asked.

"With her allergies, and what not."

Tammy continued, "Do you think she had trouble breathing that night? Shanann freaked out, did something, and then didn't want to live without her baby girl?"

"No."

Tammy continued, "Did you hear about the homicide that happened in Aurora? The guy beat his family to death with a ball-peen hammer. The only person that survived was the three year old, and she actually grew up to be a total mess. No family, no mom, no sister. She was all by herself. She said she wished she would have died with them. There are times when people freak out. I've seen it. I've been in law enforcement for almost twenty years. I've seen parents freak out, and they are, like, 'oh my God, I can't have my baby girls living without each other. They are best friends. They are like twins. They wake each other up in the morning'. I understand that. We had a mom in Castle Rock who suffocated both of her baby girls. She said her husband was going to take them, and she thought she was doing right by them. She thought she was saving them pain, and I get it," Tammy shared the story. Chris was becoming increasingly more uncomfortable as he processed what she was saying.

"How was she saving them pain?" Chris quietly asked.

"She didn't want them to have to live without their mom."

"Chris this is a weight that is going to be with you for the rest of your life, until we resolve it tonight. Unless we can resolve this, it will be with you forever. I promise, when you start to tell us, you will feel better. I know you already feel better about getting the Nikki situation off your chest," Graham added.

"Please don't involve her in the news or anything."

"You've got to help me," Graham continued.

"We are giving you a lifeline right now, please take it. You need to reach out and take it," Tammy stated.

Graham moved the picture of the girls closer to Chris. "Did they look like this the last night you were with them?"

"She had that dress on. I remember it had the two buttons on the back. I took them off when I laid them down that night."

"Did you make sure they were warm when you left the house?"

"Make sure they are warm? They're always warm. When they are in their beds, they are always warm," Chris assured, adamantly defending his parenting.

"Were you taking care of them at the very end?"

"They are always taken care of. They never missed a meal!"

"Chris, you took them out of the house with their blankets, and their animals," Tammy said with a big smile. "That's because you cared."

"I mean, I'm always caring for these kids. They are my life."

"I believe that. I believe that, and I believe someone made a mistake, whether it was you, or Shanann. You either cleaned up after Shanann, or you made the mistake. I want to believe that maybe Shanann did it and you felt compelled to fix it, so Shanann doesn't look bad. That's what I want to believe. I don't know what you aren't telling me, so it makes me think the worse. Did you take all three of them?"

"I didn't do anything to those kids, I didn't."

"What did Shanann do to them? Tell us Chris. Chicks are crazy," Tammy continued to provoke Chris, hoping he would reveal where his wife and daughters were. She and Graham were determined to find out.

"Can I talk to my dad or something?" Chris sounded mentally exhausted.

"Absolutely, do you want me to bring him in here?" Graham asked.

"Ah, I just want to talk to my dad. He flew across the country." Chris's voice was very emotional, as he asked for his dad, his hero, his rock.

"How about this? If we bring your dad in here, will you please tell him what happened?" Graham negotiated.

"I've been in here for, like, five or six hours and I'm..." Chris began wringing his hands and looking up at the ceiling, feeling the intense pressure of the situation.

"Absolutely, I understand. Chris I mean that. But, it's not going to feel any better. He deserves an answer," Graham appealed to Chris's bond with his father.

Chris took his glasses off, and wiped tears from his eyes.

"He's your best friend," Tammy said tenderly.

"There is only one person you want in here, the most, and that's your dad?" Graham stated.

"Yes."

"What would you tell him?"

"That I love him, and I just want him to be by my side," Chris stated quietly.

"Okay, he knows more than we do about you, and I think he would tell you to do the right thing. Before we get him…"

Chris interrupted, "Can I go out there and talk to him?"

"Well I don't think you want to do it out there because there are a lot of people going through the halls. Should we bring him in here?"

"We'll step out," Tammy offered. "Do you need a few minutes with him?"

Chris nodded yes.

"Okay, can we just ask a couple more questions? It seems like you are about to get it off your chest. Is there any way that you can help us understand more about Shanann, and why something happened so we don't get a bad picture about her? What happened that night with her?" Graham continued.

"You mean when I talked to her?" Chris asked.

"With the girls."

"When we were having that conversation in bed?"

"Yeah."

"When I talked to her about the separation, and the house, she asked me about the affair, and that is how that conversation went. She had mascara running down her face, all that, and it was emotional."

"Well, how about this, if we bring in your dad, will you promise me that you'll talk to him? Would it be easier if you told him and he told us? I don't know if that will be easier or not, but I think you are the type of guy who needs to take responsibility. You always have taken responsibility. I guess I'm just worried if we bring your dad in here it could distract you. What do you think?"

"Distract me from talking to you?"

"Yeah."

"I just want to talk to my dad," Chris's voice was shaking as his emotions finally slipped into the room.

"Okay, I know you'll do the right thing. I don't know how long it's going to take. I think you need to think a bit more about that, okay?" Graham assured.

"Tammy added, "You do realize that your dad is not going to stop loving you, no matter what you tell him? You are his child and he will not stop loving you, ever!"

"This is not the last chapter in anyone's story, at all! He's been here the whole time. He didn't want to leave. Have you ever seen that sometimes when an animal's owner dies, they stick around forever? I think that's your dad. Poor guy didn't want to leave today. So, keep that in mind. He wants to hear it all," Graham added.

Tammy and Graham left the room. Chris removed his glasses, wiped tears from his eyes with his sleeve, and put his glasses back on. He couldn't wait for a moment without questions but the silence in the room was heavy. The relentless tick, tick, tick, was competing with the sound of Chris's heartbeat. He wasn't certain which was which. He stared silently at the photo of his girls that was lying on the table. After several minutes Chris put his hands up, and leaned his head against them. Finally, after what seemed an eternity Ronnie, Chris's dad, entered the room. He towered over his son. Chris sat quietly looking small and defeated. Ronnie reached down and gave Chris a reassuring pat on his back. His presence filled the room, as he sat next to Chris. His expression was apprehensive, yet sympathetic, toward his son.

"Hey Chris we're going to let you have as much time as you need, okay?" Graham assured.

"Are you going to leave us in here?" Chris asked.

"Yes," Graham replied, as he and Tammy left the room.

Ronnie leaned in and quietly spoke to Chris. "Are you going to tell me what's going on son?"

"The polygraph, I failed it," Chris confessed.

"Too much emotion?"

"I mean, they're not going to let me go."

"Is there any reason why they shouldn't?"

"They know I had an affair."

"They know you had an affair?"

"Yeah."

"Anything else you want to tell me? What's going on, or do you know anything?"

"When we had that conversation, in the morning, it was emotional. I told her I wanted a separation and everything," Chris explained to his dad.

Ronnie sat listening intently to his son. "What happened after that?"

"I went downstairs and…" Chris covered his face with his hands as he agonized over his next words.

"I don't want to protect her."

"What?"

"I don't want to protect her. I don't know what else to say. She hurt them," Chris stated quietly.

"She hurt them?" Ronnie asked.

Chris whispered to his father, "And then I hurt her."

"You hurt her? But, did they leave after that, or what happened?" Ronnie asked.

Chris was silent.

"So, she started hurting the kids?" Ronnie pressed.

Chris whispered, "She smothered them."

"She smothered, or choked them?"

"I didn't hear anything, and then I came back up, and they were gone."

Ronnie put his hands to his face. It was too much to comprehend.

"I was talking to her about separation and everything, and…"

"She lost it?" Ronnie asked.

"I don't know what else to say. I freaked out and had to do the same fucking thing to her. Those were my kids."

"So, you were ready to go to work and she freaked out over the separation, and then what?"

"She laid back down, and then I heard a commotion upstairs, but I didn't think anything of it."

"Then you went back upstairs, and…" Ronnie paused.

"I could see, like, she was on top of CeCe."

"What choking her? Did she kill them?"

"They were blue."

"Both of them? She choked both of them to death?"

"I freaked out, understand me."

"Oh my God," Ronnie whispered in disbelief and despair.

Chris went on, "I don't know what to say. I don't know what to say to them. I didn't call the cops or anything."

"So what did you do? Did you haul the bodies off, or something?"

Chris nodded yes. "I didn't know what else to do."

"So she killed both CeCe and Bella, choked them to death, and then you lost it and choked her?"

"It was rage, I…" Chris slumped his head in despair.

Ronnie wiped his hand over his mustache and leaned toward the table. "God almighty son." He reached over and held Chris's arm. The clock was the only sound in the room. Ronnie rubbed his forehead, as he tried to process the situation. "I'm so sorry. God!" Ronnie exclaimed.

"In her heart, she knew about the affair, but she was waiting for me to say something, for me to deny it again, and then she just lost it," Chris explained.

"So, this happened after you told her about the affair?"

"I didn't tell her, she just knew."

"So she killed both of her children because of a separation, and an affair? I thought you told her before, and she wanted to go to counseling?" Ronnie was filled with despair as the words forced their way through his lips. The magnitude of the situation hung between father and son like a dark cloud. Ronnie wiped his brow and held his hand over his mouth, "Oh my God."

Chris looked off in the distance, as if processing what he had finally exposed. "This is the last time."

"For what, son?"

"The last time I will ever see the light of day, again," Chris almost choked on the words.

"Mercy. She lost it over the separation and…"

Chris interrupted, "She always knew, but we denied it."

"And then she killed her children!" Ronnie's voice reflected an unspeakably deep sorrow.

Tammy and Graham entered the room. Tammy placed her hand on Chris's back and asked if he was okay? She rubbed his back for a few seconds consoling him, even though it was clearly uncomfortable for him.

"Are you okay? Are you sure?" Tammy asked. She sat in the chair across from Ronnie, and Graham sat next to her. All three looked at Chris, with deep sadness.

"Will you tell us what you told your dad?" Tammy asked.

"After that conversation we had, she accused me of the affair, and in her heart she knew what was going on. She knew about the dinner the other night. It cost too much for just me."

"Did you tell her?" Ronnie asked.

"I told her I went to a Rockies game. Then I went downstairs and started packing up a few things, and I heard a couple things upstairs, but I didn't think anything of it. Tammy and Ronnie both put their hands on Chris's shoulders offering him support, as he continued. Chris was clearly uncomfortable, trapped by hands on either side of him, trapped within the small room, trapped by actions that were now closing in on him.

"I went upstairs to talk to her again and saw the monitor. Bella's covers were pulled off and she was just lying there. So I went into CeCe's room and Shanann was on top of her. I freaked out and got on top of Shanann."

"What did you do?" Tammy asked. The clock was suddenly too loud for the room, tick, tick, tick!

"Those were my babies," Chris stated.

"What happened next?" Tammy prompted.

"I had no idea what to do. I was shaking. Both my kids are gone. I'm not that person. She hurt my kids. I did the same thing to her."

"What happened after you got off the bed?"

"I didn't know what to do. I just covered her up. They're gone. There is no bringing them back," The words stung as he spoke them. The finality of the loss was bleeding through Chris's shock.

"Where are they?" Tammy asked.

Ronnie continued to rub Chris's shoulder, offering him comfort.

"They are at that first location I went to that day," Chris confessed.

Tammy pulled over a map of area 319, the Anadarko location. "Where will we find them?"

"Right there," Chris pointed out the location on the map. "I didn't know what to do," Chris stated quietly. His voice was breaking.

"I know," Tammy said gently.

"I didn't know what to do," Chris raised his voice and then finally broke down. "None of this made sense. Why would she fucking hurt my girls?" Chris asked as he choked on his tears.

"Chris, did you put them in something? Are they under the ground? Where we will find them? Can you take us out there?" Tammy asked.

"I don't want to go back there." Chris's voice was filled with pain. "I mean I will if you want me to," Chris stated in desperation, openly crying.

"What if you and your dad just drove by and you could just point and say 'right there'? We can help you get them out of the cold. Take care of them for the last time."

"I'm sorry," Chris continued crying, and wiping the tears from his eyes.

"I know," Tammy consoled. "I know you came in today to do the right thing. You didn't have to come in. You came in all on your own."

Chris put his head in his hands and wept out loud. "Please don't think anything less of me."

Ronnie quickly responded. "I won't. Are all three of them out there Chris?"

"Yes."

"What was she doing to CeCe?" Tammy asked again.

"She was just on top of her."

"You saw her?" Graham asked.

"I saw it on the monitor. That's why I ran in there."

"What did you say?" Tammy asked.

"I told her to get off. I saw that CeCe was turning blue and not moving. I was so full of blind rage, I did the same thing to her."

"Did you go into Bella's room?"

"I saw her the monitor, the way she was laying, all sprawled out."

"Is that when you packed up your stuff? So where did you put them to get them out there?" Tammy asked.

"In the truck. My babies are gone. I put my hands around my wife's neck and did that same thing." Chris was completely distraught.

"Did Shanann fight back, at all?" Tammy asked.

"I had so much rage after seeing that. No, not much!"

"How do you know Shanann was dead?" Tammy asked. There was a long silence. Ronnie spoke up, "If you look at Shanann's Facebook page, about two days ago, there was a long, four or five foot doll laying with a sheet over its head. All you could see was where the feet were hanging out. Shanann said Bella had done that. A kid wouldn't do that."

"Shanann posted it?" Graham asked.

"Yeah, it said something like, 'I don't know what to think about this'. She said Bella had done that," Ronnie explained.

"Do you remember that Chris? What do you think?" Graham asked.

"She made fun of it. She thought it was funny."

"Did Bella do it?" Tammy joined in the conversation. A life-size doll laying on the sofa with a sheet over its head seemed odd.

"I don't know," Chris answered.

"I don't think so. It doesn't seem like Bella would do something like that, to cover up the head like that."

There was a long pause in the room. Chris looked at Tammy and Graham, "I'm sorry I lied to you. I mean, you knew what was going to happen," Chris said with conviction.

Tammy consoled Chris with a pat on the shoulder. "Yep, you stayed for a reason."

"Chris you're a good man," Graham added.

"I'm not a good man," Chris stated.

"You stayed, you wanted to talk, you knew it was going to be hard, and you still stayed. That's what a good man is."

"Obviously rage would come out when you see your kids like that," Ronnie tried to comfort his son by rationalizing Chris's behavior. "You don't know. You don't know what you might do," Ronnie continued.

"You don't know," Chris said sobbing. "You don't know!" Ronnie moved closer to comfort his shattered son, as Chris mumbled his inconsolable grief. "Life will never be the same again," Chris cried.

"When you came in, was your wife still on top of CeCe? You saw it in person?" Graham asked.

"I saw it on the monitor. That's why I rushed in."

"When you came in, she was right there on top of her?"

"She was right there," Chris responded.

"She had her hands around her throat?" Ronnie asked.

Chris was weeping deeply.

"Did you try and save CeCe?" Graham asked.

"She had her hands over her face, like this." Chris spoke through his tears and put his hands together to show Graham.

Tammy turned the conversation back to the missing bodies. "Chris, where did you put them? That's really important."

Chris reached for a tissue to wipe his eyes. He shook his hands in frustration.

"I didn't know what to do. I was so scared."

"I know," Tammy consoled.

"I didn't know what to do. Anything I did from then on was going to be a horrible thing." Chris took a few deep breathes and tried to regain his composure.

"Will you show your dad where they are?" Tammy asked.

"What's going to happen?" Chris asked.

"We're going to help them get out of there," Graham assured. "Would you prefer one of your co-workers go out there?"

"Oh my God no. No! I can't," Chris began sobbing again. The reality of the situation had fully sunk in. "They all think I'm a good man. They're going to see this, and say 'what the fuck did you do man'?"

"Well, they aren't living your life, or walking in your shoes, so they don't know," Tammy offered.

"I know, but I can't have anyone out there show you around, I can't," Chris stated emphatically.

Tammy looked at Graham.

"Okay, we'll take this one step at a time," Graham consoled.

"I mean, they are going to form their own opinions of me anyway. They are going to figure everything out anyway." Chris seemed to understand that this was no longer a secret that he was sharing. Tammy, Graham, Ronnie, his family, friends, co-workers, the world was going to know about this situation. Chris was devastated by the idea.

"We'll just take small steps now, okay?"

"Is anyone out there?" Chris asked.

"No, we are waiting for you. Can you, and me, Tammy and Ronnie just get in the car and drive out there?" Graham asked.

"Chris, I know they're gone, but they are still your babies," Tammy added.

Chris sobbed deeply.

"You don't want anyone else to find them out there. You don't, I promise you. So do you want us to get things arranged?" Tammy and Graham stood up to leave the room. Graham squeezed Chris's shoulder as he walked out.

"I don't know what the fuck to do," Chris admitted to Ronnie, sobbing "This is just fucking horrible. I don't know if they even believe me or not."

"That's your wife out there son."

"Mom said she was a terrible person, but I never thought anything like this would happen," Chris tried to rationalize.

"Maybe she just lost herself," Ronnie offered.

"How can this happen to those two little girls?" Chris questioned.

Ronnie was at a loss for words. There was nothing he could say to make this right. "I'm so sorry son!" There was a long pause in the room.

"She did something stupid," Ronnie tried to rationalize.

"I emotionally drove her to do something stupid," Chris reflected.

"I guess the situation triggered that. Don't blame yourself for that."

"That's all I can do right now," Chris admitted.

"Don't blame yourself for that Chris. There is no reason she should have done that, no reason to kill her children." Ronnie, deeply saddened, tried to console his child while grieving for his granddaughters, and attempting to understand his daughter in-law. "It's a crime of passion, we'll figure it out," Ronnie added.

"I hid it," Chris stated.

"They will realize what you just lived through."

"I hid it. That is the thing. I didn't call the police when it happened."

"You were confused about what to do. It's not good, but we'll get you a lawyer and figure out what to do with the house," Ronnie reassured.

"It's already going on the market. Shanann emailed the relator and then I called her Monday."

Ronnie was overwhelmed by the situation. This didn't make sense. "Shanann's good with the kids."

"She has a temper. She's had that. One minute she's okay and then she's not," Chris explained.

"She knew about the separation before, why?"

"She knew about the affair," Chris interrupted, trying to explain Shanann to his dad.

Ronnie and Chris picked up their phones. They needed a deterrent, a moment of reprieve, from the intense emotion that had built up in the small room. The clock was relentless, tick, tick, tick.

Ronnie began rubbing Chris's back again while they waited for the detectives to come back into the room. "You were reacting to the one who killed both your children."

"That doesn't make it right."

"I know that. I'm not making excuses for you, but, it seems that whether you called the police, or not, is neither here nor there."

Chris broke into tears again, "I just ruined your life. I ruined my life. I ruined everybody's life. I ruined Jamie's life. I ruined what all my friend's think. I've ruined everything. Do you think I should call my foreman? Should I call my foreman?"

"You mean about going up there now?" Ronnie asked.

"Yeah."

"Can you tell us, basically, where it's at?" Ronnie asked.

"No, too many turns," Chris said

"Do you think you can go there and show us where it's at?"

"That's what I feel horrible about. They're in a freaking oil tank. I didn't know what else to do. Please God forgive me. Dad I just wanted to tell you first."

Ronnie continued to rub Chris's back as he suffered every parent's worst nightmare. There was no way to ease his son's pain. This was bigger than his family. This was bigger than the years he had spent protecting his boy. This was literally life and death.

"They're gone! They're gone!" Chris yelled out in desperation. Chris took a deep breath and tried to calm down, Ronnie still rubbing his shoulders.

"I knew it was going to happen, coming in here today. I've never taken a polygraph before, but I knew it was going to happen," Chris confessed.

"Ah, son, son, son!"

"I've been in here a long time," Chris stated.

The bond between Chris and Ronnie was evident. There was no need for words. Tammy   and Graham entered the room.

"Can I use the bathroom and text my wife? This isn't going to be on the news anytime soon is it?" Ronnie asked. *God, I don't want Cindy to hear this on the news.*

"Not tonight. I really don't have any say in that. Do you want me to show you out?" Tammy offered.

"Yeah, I think I'll go outside for a few minutes." Ronnie needed a breath of fresh air. He needed to process what his son had just told him. His daughter-in-law and his beautiful granddaughters were gone. And now he had to tell his wife. He shook his head in heavy sorrow, as he tried to process the situation.

"Watch for the press out there," Tammy suggested.

"We are going to try and keep this, ah, we don't gain anything by broadcasting to the press. That's not what law enforcement is really about. We will try our best to handle this as discretely as possible," Graham offered, as Ronnie left the room.

"So, we are going to talk a little bit more. I think we have a picture of Cervi 319. We are going to walk you through that. I'm sure you have a ton of questions for us, about how your night is going to look." Tammy showed Chris the overhead picture of the Anadarko work site, "Does that look familiar to you?"

"Yeah, it's site 319," Chris confirmed.

"Where are Shanann and the girls?"

"How old is this picture?" Chris asked.

"Today."

"Oh, this is today?" Chris sounded surprised.

Tammy handed Chris a pen. "Can you mark it for me?

Chris took the photo and marked a small mound of dirt.

"Is that "S" for Shanann?"

Chris nodded yes.

"And where are the girls?" Tammy asked.

"They are in here." Chris pointed to two large oil tanks.

"In these? Do you know which one?" Tammy managed to maintain her composure even though the optics were unthinkable.

"Are they in the tanks? Does someone have to know what they are doing to open those tanks?" Graham asked.

"What's in the tanks?" Tammy inquired.

"A mixture of oil and water," Chris answered.

"There was a sheet found down here? Where was that from?" Tammy asked.

"Shanann was wrapped in it," Chris answered.

"What about the girls? What were the girls wrapped in?" Tammy continued.

"Nothing."

"So, how did you dig that?" Tammy asked, referring to the shallow grave where Chris said he put his wife.

"I had a shovel in the back of my truck."

"Was it a work shovel? Is it still there?" Chris nodded yes to her questions. Tammy continued, "How was Shanann dressed?"

"Shirt, and underwear," Chris said quietly.

"Is that what she wore to bed?'

"Yeah, I think her shirt was black or gray, and her underwear was blue."

"How much time passed from when she got back into bed, until you put them in the truck?" Graham asked.

"I'm not sure."

"Are we talking minutes, hours?"

"You mean when I left the house?"

"When you were in the bed, until you put her in the truck. How long was that?"

"From the bed, to the truck?" Chris asked.

"Yeah, from your master bed to the truck? Is there anything else you have left in certain spots? Are you sure their blankets and toys aren't going to be out there as well?"

Chris nodded no. He indicated on the picture where he dug a shallow grave to bury his wife and his unborn son, and he marked the tanks that held his daughter's tiny bodies. Tammy asked him to sign the picture, and she dated it, 8/15/18, 5:56. She left the room.

"Was your wife wearing any shorts, or pants, or just underwear?" Graham asked.

"Just underwear."

"What color?"

"Blue."

"And the girls, what color pajamas were they wearing?"

"They both had on nightgowns. Celeste had a pink one with bears on it. I think Bella's had a unicorn on it."

"So, it sounds to me like we know pretty well how to go and get them. What else do we need to know?"

"About how to get them?" Chris asked.

"Yeah. Do we have to climb to the top, unscrew something, and then lower something down to get them?"

"There is a hatch on the top. They are twenty foot tanks. Do you want me to go out there?"

"I don't think so. Would you prefer not to?"

"I don't know, if you need help getting there," Chris stated.

"I think once we got that picture, we really didn't know as much as about the location, as the police officers knew. It sounds like they knew how to get to the right spot, Cervi 319. That's how they got that picture. You have a nanny-cam right?"

"No, it's just a monitor."

"Does it record?" Graham asked.

"No."

"I'm just wondering what you think made Shanann snap?" Graham asked.

"Knowing that I had an affair. She just knew. I didn't admit it."

Tammy walked back into the room and sat down.

"We were just getting into why Chris thinks Shanann snapped. He thinks she was distressed, about the other woman." Graham brought Tammy into the conversation.

"Knowing, but she didn't really know right?" Tammy asked.

"In her heart she knew. She just wanted me to admit it."

"Can we talk about a couple of tough things? I think we need to get it out of the way. Get it out, to make sure you have every chance to tell us what happened, and we can ask questions. So the conversation happened. You go downstairs and she is upstairs. You saw what?"

"I just heard a commotion upstairs. I heard like a bang, but I didn't think anything of it. I was just packing everything up, getting ready to go. I went back up to talk to her in the master bedroom. She wasn't in there."

"You went there first, and why did you go up again?" Graham asked.

"I wanted to talk to her again."

"So, that noise didn't make you run up?"

"No, it didn't even register with me. I looked at the monitor that was on Bella."

"Where is the screen you looked at? Is it upstairs or downstairs?"

"It's upstairs."

"Okay, so you go upstairs and you see the monitor?"

"Yeah, it's in our bedroom. I could see Bella. Her covers were pulled back and she was sprawled out, just lying there. There are four or five second intervals before the view cycles, and then it cycled over to CeCe in her room. That's when I saw Shanann on top of her. That's when I ran in."

"Okay, can we talk about something very difficult? It's important that we understand. We don't want anything to be incorrect, or inaccurate. Was your wife on top of CeCe? What did that look like? Was she straddling her?"

"Yeah," Chris stated quietly.

"And where were they?"

"On the bed."

Graham held his hands out as if he were strangling someone. "Was she doing something like this?"

"I walked up from the back and yeah it looked like that."

"Was CeCe face up, or face down?"

"She was laying on her side. That's when I pulled Shanann off CeCe. She was limp and blue."

"And then what happened?"

"I looked at her, then I got on top of Shanann and did the same thing."

"Did you have to knock her down?"

"No."

"She was already on the ground?"

"I just pulled her on the bed. I lost it."

"And where was Shanann?"

"On the bed. She was on top of CeCe, and I saw what was happening, and I pulled her over on the bed."

"What size is the bed, full, queen?" Tammy asked.

"It's probably a queen." Chris got his phone out and pulled up a picture of CeCe's bed.

Tammy looked at it. "So where was Celeste?"

"She was at the top. Then I pulled Shanann down cross ways."

"Was your daughter on this side, or that side, looking at the picture?" Graham asked.

"CeCe usually sleeps in the middle."

"Your wife was right on top of her? Which way did you pull her?"

Chris showed Graham the left side of the bed in the photo.

"Did she put up a fight?" Graham inquired.

"It didn't feel like she did."

"Was she yelling? Was she screaming? Was she talking? Was she scratching you?"

"I felt such anger. I didn't feel anything else. If she did, nothing shows on me."

"Was it quick? Was it slow? Was it?"

Chris interrupted, "I don't know, it felt like it was fast."

"Is it possible that her neck is broken?"

"I've never broken a bone, so I don't know."

"Were you choking with your hands, or was it a headlock?" Tammy asked Chris to show how his hands were positioned. "And your wife, was she using one hand or two hands?" Tammy brought the questioning back to Shanann and CeCe.

"I was looking from the back, and I couldn't really tell. The monitor isn't in color, its black and white."

"Between when you finished talking to Shanann, and when you found her with CeCe, did you have any inkling that she was going to do something?" Tammy asked.

"We both love those kids more than you could know. And my family has always said she was unstable. My friends said she was unstable, but I never would have thought."

"Who said she was unstable?" Tammy asked.

"My family. My friend Mark. People that I've seen her around."

"Well, Chris, this doesn't look good, I'm not going to lie. It actually looks pretty bad," Tammy stated.

"Is it possible, when we get the girls, we are going to see the cause of death as anything other than her hands?" Graham asked.

"No."

"And what I mean by that, and I want to be very clear, some of us find it hard to believe that your wife did it. You can imagine that, okay? So is it possible that maybe she did one, and then you did Shanann, and then you did your other daughter?" Graham continued.

"No, no."

"Is there any other way that we might see your hands on the girl's necks?"

"No, lord no."

"You know when we find their little bodies, we are going to see the diameter of someone's hands, and someone's fingers on their necks. Is it possible we are going to see yours? I know it's hard and I know you are probably getting angry at my questions, but we have to ask."

There was a long pause. Chris sat silently.

"What are you thinking about Chris?" Tammy asked.

"That I let my family down. I let my dad down, my mom, sister, nephews, nieces, friends, co-workers."

"Can I ask a tough question? Can we just get it all on the table? When you see Shanann choking, strangling Celeste, and you pull her off of Celeste, did you think about calling an ambulance?"

"I've never seen anything like that in my life. I mean she wasn't moving at all. No gasp, no breath, totally just blue."

"So Chris, I know a lot about psychology and how people react. Most parents wouldn't even fathom that their child was dead. Even if their kid is stiff, blue, and has been dead all night, they still call an ambulance to see if someone can revive their child. And the ambulance gets there, and they confirm that the child has been dead all night, the parents are still frantic, in denial, and they still want something done to help their child. That's why I want you to explain to me what was going on in your head."

"When I saw what she did, rage just took over."

Tammy looked at him with confusion.

"I can see where you are coming from," Chris admitted. There was another long pause.

"I would hate for Shanann to get a bad rap if she didn't have anything to do with this. It's not fair."

"I know."

"Enough bad stuff has happened. And we need to just stop the bad stuff from happening. Do you just want to tell me the truth?"

"That is the truth." Chris answered quietly while staring at Tammy.

"I just want to make sure. So you're good with the public knowing that Shanann killed your daughters?"

"Yes, because I did not hurt these girls."

"Chris, I'm not sure I believe you," Graham added.

Tammy went on, "I don't think you meant to."

"I didn't hurt them."

"You didn't save them either, you know?" Tammy pointed out.

"I know that," Chris acknowledged.

"That doesn't make sense either," Tammy stated.

"None of this makes sense. Why would she do that? None of this makes sense," Chris proclaimed.

"Are you sure Shanann didn't catch you hurting the girls?" Graham asked.

"No, oh God, no."

"Chris, you can imagine that we're pretty cynical in our jobs. We've had to talk a lot about various things, and don't get mad, but what it looks like, is you found a new life and the only way to get that new life was to get rid of the old one. And I think that you killed these girls before their mom came home, and then killed Shanann," Graham stated.

"No," Chris whispered.

"That's what we are left with, what we have to believe, because it just doesn't make sense. I mean to Tammy's point, if I walked in and my kid was decapitated, I would still call an ambulance."

"Knowing there is no hope," Tammy added.

"It just doesn't add up. So, either you're this monster, who just wants this young hot girlfriend, and kills everyone to see how it works out, and if you're not that monster, I think we are very close to the truth," Graham let the words sit in the room.

"I'm not a monster. I didn't kill my babies."

"Okay, so, tell us what actually happened."

"I told you what happened."

"You know we are getting later into the day. We've gone through this a few times, we talk, and then we show you some evidence we are working on, facts we uncover while we are making our way to the truth."

"Everything I've told you is the truth."

"So what's going to happen when the cause of death comes back to you?"

"It's not going to."

"Okay, are you sure?" Graham asked.

"I'm 100% positive, it's not going to come back to me."

"Who's it going to come back to?"

"Shanann was on top of CeCe. What do you want me to say?" Chris asked in a whisper.

"I just want the truth."

"That is the truth," Chris softly said.

"What about Bella?"

"Bella was laid out, sprawled out on her bed. And I saw Shanann on top of CeCe so I ran in there." Chris explained.

"Okay, and what happens when a coroner looks and says the finger prints on their necks are yours?"

"They're not going to be my finger prints." Chris said with confidence.

"Who will they be the prints of?" Graham continued to grill Chris searching for the truth.

"It's going to be Shanann," Chris responded.

"Are you sure? But we don't know about Bella, right?'

"Bella, ah, I heard the commotion upstairs and I'm assuming." Chris sounded confused.

"Why did you take their bodies out of the house and bury them?"

"I was scared. I didn't know what else to do. Nothing, nothing was going to...
I didn't know what else to do. I honestly didn't know what else to do."

"Scared of what?" Graham asked.

"Afraid of what everything was going to look like. My two babies are gone and I just did that to my wife. I was the only one in the house. What did you expect was going to happen?"

"It did look bad, right?" Graham confirmed.

"A nightmare," Chris gasped the answer.

"Okay, even with any problems you had with Shanann, at the end of the day, she was a pretty good mom, right?"

"I was a pretty good dad, as well. You don't know a person until you don't know a person."

"I would hate for a woman, who can't defend herself..." Tammy paused and went on, "If you aren't being truthful about who took their lives, well that reflects on the girls as well. And you don't want to do that to them," Tammy pointed out.

"I'm not doing that to them."

"I'm just saying," Tammy stated.

Chris looked at Tammy directly, "I'm not doing that to them," he stated aggressively.

"I think you were a good dad, but I think Shanann was a good mom. I think you guys were doing everything that you could possibly do for those girls." Tammy pointed to the picture of the girls. "I mean look at them."

"Why didn't you put Shanann in the tanks?"

"I didn't know what else to do."

"How far down is she?" Tammy asked about Shanann's shallow grave.

"I don't know, like two feet maybe." Chris slipped back into his passive demeanor.

"How long did it take you to dig that?"

"I don't know." Chris sighed with exhaustion.

"Give me an idea," Tammy pushed.

"Twenty, to thirty minutes."

"Does anyone ever go up this ladder and look in the tanks?"

"Yeah."

"So how were you going to avoid that, or is it you that does that?"

"Anybody can look in the tanks," Chris confirmed.

"How often are they checked?" Tammy inquired.

"It depends if their making enough oil or not. A week maybe."

"So, did you want someone to find them?" Tammy asked.

"I didn't know what else to do. That was the location I was going out to that morning. I didn't know what else to do."

"So you weren't thinking that far ahead?"

"No," Chris stated emphatically.

"Yesterday when you were talking, before we got to this moment today, you said you didn't know where they were. You said something like, whatever happened to them was an act of pure evil. What did you mean by that?" Graham asked Chris.

"The evil that I saw when I walked in and saw Shanann on top of CeCe. And I thought what I did to Shanann was evil."

"Okay, there is one other thing that doesn't make sense to me. Can you walk me through this again? When you walked in the room, what did Shanann look like? All you saw was her back? Was it the same shirt that you buried her in? Same underwear? Was she wearing pajamas?"

"Shanann? No, that's what she sleeps in. She sleeps in her underwear," Chris stated.

"Okay, no pajamas, no shorts, nothing like that?"

"So, did Shanann even go to bed when she got home? After she got home and then you woke her up at 4:00, in that time, it looks like there were some hair care products purchased early in the morning. A credit card purchase was denied. Would you have bought hair care products at 2:30 in the morning?" Tammy asked.

"No."

"Did she get mad at you because there was no money when she woke up? Was that part of it?"

"No, that's the first I've heard about that and the credit card being denied," Chris stated.

"Is there any reason she would have a black eye?"

"No."

"Not from a punch, or a slap, or anything?" Graham asked.

"No, I've never punched her, or slapped her."

"Is there any reason she would have a stab mark on her body?"

"No."

"No other reason for death? The coroner isn't going to find rat poison in her stomach?"

"No."

"There is only one way she died? She was living and breathing until your hands were on her neck."

"Yeah," Chris confessed.

Tammy joined the conversation. "What were you talking to Nikki about, before your wife came home?"

"Before she got home?" Chris asked.

"You talked for several hours," Tammy pointed out.

"We talked a lot, just conversations."

"Does Nikki know about any of this?"

"I mean she knows from the news and everything like that."

"Did she know your wife was pregnant?"

"She does now. I told her that," Chris explained.

"She didn't know at the time. Why didn't you tell her?"

"I was afraid to. I felt like she wouldn't have gone on a date with me if she knew that."

"Did she know you were married, with kids?" Graham asked.

"Yes."

"Just not pregnant?"

"She knew Shanann and I actively tried to get pregnant before Nikki and I met."

"You can imagine, when we go and talk to people, everyone is going to distance themselves from any of this," Graham stated.

"Yes."

"And, what happens when Nikki says, 'no, it was our plan to kill everyone and run off together'?"

"She's not going to say that," Chris insisted.

"Okay."

"Are you going to talk to her?" Chris asked

"Absolutely," Graham declared.

"We have to," Tammy explained.

"So, can we get ahead of that for you? Are you sure she isn't going to say she kind of knew you were going to kill them?" Graham inquired.

"She isn't going to say that."

"And, is she going to say you two were making plans about buying a house or an apartment?"

"No, once I had my own place we were going to hang out more."

"So, after the separation, after that dust settled, you would have more time to see Nikki. Did you talk about that?"

"Yeah, she genuinely liked me. Please don't put her name out there in the news though. She's been through enough in her life."

"We try not to put out any information like that."

"If the media knew we were having an affair they would drag her through the mud and I don't want that," Chris insisted.

"We're certainly not going to try and do that."

"So what do you think about everything now? Do you feel sorry for what you did?" Tammy asked.

"Of course, if I wouldn't have lost control and then done that." Chris was silent for a long time.

Graham finally interrupted, "So after they get their bodies, we are going to have a lot more questions. Things will be different then, but we would love to talk to you at that time as well. You've done really good Chris.

I think you've had twenty-four hours of a hellish nightmare thrust upon you. I think that you made it better today."

"I think you were here for a reason," Tammy reassured.

"There was a reason I came in. I knew this was going to happen."

"We appreciate that. Chris you know what they are going to find out there. If you were just sitting at home waiting for that to happen, then what? What does that look like? There are a lot of people who say you are an amazing guy, and you would never do anything bad, and you would never lose your temper. All those people that would say that about you. There are just as many who would say that about Shanann. So we're going to struggle with that for a while. I'm struggling with that right now. I'm a mom."

"I know, anybody would," Chris offered.

"How do we prove that Shanann did it?" Graham asked.

"Examine the body, I guess."

"Are there going to be hand-marks?" Tammy asked. "Why were there sheets in the trash?"

"They were the same ones out there. I didn't know what to do. I knew eventually they were going to find Shanann," Chris acknowledged.

"Was she still wrapped in the sheet, when you put her in the ground?"

"No, it was laying off to the side. Maybe the wind took it."

Tammy pointed to the picture of the job site. "So it's here, right now? So you didn't even try to hide that?"

"I was so scared, I didn't know what to do."

"Did someone come up on you or something?" Graham asked.

"No."

"Were you afraid the crew was going to start showing up?" Tammy inquired

"I knew they were on their way out there."

Tammy requested all of the passwords for any electronics in the house, and information regarding their banking information. Chris gave them passwords to the phones, computers, and the security system. One of the passwords seemed odd to Tammy. "What is the date for this one?"

"It is Shanann's ex-husband's birthday. They remained good friends and Shanann never changed the password."

"Do you have any questions for us?"

"I need to go to the bathroom."

"We need to do one more thing. Now that we know what we know, we need to make sure you don't have any weapons on you. Do you have any weapons on you?"

"No."

"Then go to the bathroom. I'm not going in the stall with you, but I am going with you. Then we will come back here and make a decision about how the rest of the night goes."

Chris stood up so Graham could check him for weapons, and they went to the bathroom. When Chris and Graham returned to the room, Graham took Chris's phone and wallet. "We're are going to make a decision on your belongings, but I'm going to take them with me now."

Graham left the room as Chris sat silently waiting. As the hour passed, a fear of the future crept into the room like a silent mist. Chris knew this was an ending. He wouldn't sleep in his bed tonight. He wouldn't read to the girls. He wouldn't say good night to his wife. Life as he knew it was gone, forever! The door opened and an unfamiliar voice entered the room.

"Chris, do you want to stand up for me? I'm going to have you face that wall. Just face it. Lift up your hands," the police officer directed. He placed a belt around Chris's waist and secured it. Chris faced the officer while he put him in handcuffs. He secured the handcuffs to the belt. "You don't have anything on you right?"

"No."

"Okay, I'm going to search you all right? Face away from me and spread your legs. Turn around and face me. No earrings, necklaces, anything like that?"

"No." Chris was escorted down a narrow hall to the garage of the station. He climbed into the back seat of the police car and into a future he had never imagined.

***

Tammy was shaking when she got home. What the hell had she just heard? She knew very well the interview process can make or break a case. It was so important to make Chris feel comfortable so he would tell the truth. There was an urgent need to get Chris's story down. It was so important they ask the right questions. Chris had seemed so calm during the interview, although he showed frustration at times when Agent Coder had pressed him. She and Agent Coder had intentionally done some victim blaming against Shanann, knowing that it might be easier for Chris to rationalize his actions. Tammy thought about the process. Shanann had the stronger personality and looking at the situation through that lens might allow Chris to open up about what had really happened. It worked. The second she had brought up the idea, that maybe Shanann had a role in the event, Chris lit up. This was the thing he wanted to go with. He wanted to put the blame on Shanann. It was horrifying to hear Chris admit to murdering his wife in front of his dad. *I can't believe he actually admitted it, even while he blamed Shanann for killing the girls.* She and Agent Coder had never worked together, but they were both skeptical when Chris wanted to see his dad. They had no idea what Ronnie would say or do. The clear objective, for them, was finding Shanann and the girls. Chris gave them an emotional account of the shallow grave he dug, and how he dumped his wife's body in it. That was horrific enough, but when he marked a 'B' and a 'C' on the oil tanks, Tammy felt physically ill. *Oh my God, oil tanks.* It was all she could do to compose herself. Finally, in the safety of her bedroom she released and collapsed to the floor, crying for Shanann, her unborn son, and those little baby girls. She was a tough CBI agent, but in that moment her heart was broken. She knew this case would always be with her.

Chapter 10

Shannon walked out of the house. When he heard the door slam, Speaks With Stars looked over and was visibly shaken at what he saw. Shanann's eyes were bloodshot. Her long hair was matted and disheveled. Her t-shirt was covered in dirt. She looked him in the eye, and the sound of her voice chilled him to the bone.

"I remember!" Shanann's voice was cold and shattered the silence. As she walked toward him, the flame of his low-burning fire suddenly went out.

"My husband, he murdered me, and he killed our children." The words tasted like bitter poison as they rolled off her tongue. She knew she was never going back to the life she once had. Chris, the man she loved, her own husband had snuffed them out, all of them. This was no dream. This was a fucking nightmare. Speaks With Stars' presence seemed to calm her and she sat down beside him. Her words were sharp as she continued, "I knew about his affair. It was like he had completely changed overnight. He found a replacement for me, and was trading me in for someone else."

Shanann sat quietly for a moment, as if she were allowing the thoughts to roll through her mind, searching for clarity, for an explanation, for anything to make sense. "When Chris put his hands around my neck, he knew exactly what to do. I was just lying there, so groggy, I could barely move. Then I was in shock. It was surreal. All I could see was the cold indifference in his eyes. He was completely disconnected from me, from our life, from reality." Shanann drifted off into silence. Her gaze was deliberate as she turned and looked at Speaks With Stars.

"What he did to me was unthinkable, but what he did to our children." Shanann paused. She was trembling with anger. "Chris knew he was going to do it. He sent me a picture of a doll covered with a sheet. I thought it was creepy, but never in a million years did I think he was planning..." Shanann couldn't finish her sentence. Her voice had changed. It was low and fierce. There was a blaze in her eyes. She didn't say a word as she walked away. Speaks With Stars relit his fire. The scent of sage filled the air as he took a long draw from his pipe. The beat of his drum was steady and deliberate. He was not surprised that Silver Moon sat by his side. Their voices filled the night sky with the healing song of their ancestors.

***

The cell was small and dark. There was only a dim ray of light for the guards to peek through. Chris was on suicide watch. He was wearing a one-piece, anti-suicide garment which was meant to deter him from using it to make a noose. The silence was deafening, but unbeknownst to Chris at the time, it was a silence he would long for. Once they moved him to the hole, his new location would offer no silence. He would find out soon enough that there was a code in prison, and killing children, especially your own, was not high on the respect list. The other prisoners were highly motivated when instructing him on how he might kill himself.

"Stick your head in the toilet. Shove a sock down your throat."

Everything was still a blur. Was it only days since he had taken the girls to a birthday party, filling up water balloons and listening to their giggles?

No pillow, no blanket, nothing, Chris was totally alone. He closed his eyes and tried to sleep.

Shanann could not see him, but she knew he was here. She could feel his presence. She wasn't sure if he would be able to hear her, but she had come for one reason, to confront the man who murdered her. Chris was lying on his bunk, hoping he might be able to sleep, maybe just an hour. This nightmare was wearing him to the bone. The long agonizing hours of questions, the police, the press, the devastated look on his dad's face when he said he strangled Shanann. The arrest, the body search, this cold dark cell. Chris thought about how he sat in the interrogation room, watching the video of the girls on his phone. He thought about them playing on the beach. CeCe flirting with the water, daring the waves, running away and screaming in delight. Bella holding his hand, ever-cautious as she analyzed the waves and kept a close eye on her little sister. Chris closed his eyes, desperately seeking a moment of solace, just a breath of peace, a few moments away from this nightmare. Finally, he drifted off.

His reprieve was short-lived as a burst of cold air shot through his body and jolted him back into the reality of his cell. Chris shook with terror. *Oh my God, someone is in this cell.* He looked over. There was a presence standing in the corner, in the darkness. He could see red eyes, and a shiver of horror shot through his entire body. He wanted to move, but he couldn't. He was paralyzed with fear. His rational mind searched for an explanation. Maybe this was someone who had died, someone from his past, someone he knew. Chris closed his eyes tightly, hoping whoever it was would go away. His body shook violently as he longed for an escape.

She whispered into the cold empty room, "I know what you did. You were having an affair. You wanted us out of your life. You wanted our removal to be tidy, uneventful, no drama. If you quietly, calmly, smothered the girls in their beds, they would simply slip away. If you gave me a bit of Oxy, I would be relaxed, and calm; straddling me, putting your hands around my throat and squeezing until my body was limp, would be easy. You stole my ability to fight back. You stole my breath. You stole my life. And when Bella came into our bedroom, your tidy little plan exploded. She saw you, not the persona of the perfect daddy, but some other part of you. She saw what you were capable of, and your simple plan turned into a living nightmare. And when she asked what was wrong with mommy, you scrambled to put all of the shattered pieces back together and you lied, 'mommy is sick'. Did panic, rage and an entire plethora of enormous emotion threaten to consume you; the excitement of having an affair, the thrill of doing it in secret, the guilt of blowing up our life, the shame of lying and hiding? Were those feelings bubbling up Chris, threatening to blow up your tidy world? Or did you feel nothing? Nothing, except the threat that everyone would see behind your cracking mask? You put plastic bags over my head and feet, and you drug me down the stairs like garbage. You put our scared, confused daughters in the back of your truck and drove for almost an hour to your work site. They clung to one another, crying, and terrified. They tried to comfort one another, but their dead mommy was lying at their feet. You dumped me in the dirt, in a shallow grave, face down. My confused body gave birth to your son. You took CeCe's favorite blanket and smothered the life out of her. You climbed a ladder and forced her little body into a small hole, listening for the sound, as she hit the oil. Bella asked if you were going to do the same thing to her and then begged you not to, 'No daddy'. You smothered the life out of her and shoved her in a separate oil tank, away from her sister. You murdered us. You killed all of us. I know what you did, because I saw you. Bella and CeCe were so confused, so scared, and I couldn't stop you. I couldn't get through to you no matter how hard I tried. I watched you murder our children."

The energy of her rage filled the entire cell. The small light outside of the cell flickered wildly. "How could you accuse me of killing the girls? You are a fucking liar and a coward." The sudden thought of the girls and her rage had zapped all of her energy, and Shanann was suddenly jolted out of her rant. She needed to find Bella.

***

Shanann woke as if from a long, tiresome, dream. *Is this my living room?* The smell of smoke was overwhelmingly nauseating. *Why am I laying on the floor?* Startled, she jumped up and looked around. Her beautiful living room was in ashes. *Oh my God, there was a fire.* She couldn't remember what had happened. Everything around her was hazy, burnt, devastated. Shanann sank into the blackened remains of her couch. Exhaustion was suddenly her only companion. She wanted to sleep forever, to just fall into a deep sense of nothingness and never wake up. Suddenly, she remembered why she was here. She remembered Chris shaking with terror in his cold dark cell. He was all alone and terrified. Is that what Bella is feeling right now? *Oh my God, where is my Bella*? She ignored the sense of hopelessness she was drowning in. Finding her daughter was the only thing that existed. Wherever she was, whatever had happened, whatever was in the next moment, the only thing that mattered was finding Bella. Shanann made her way through the burnt remains of her home to the front door. He was waiting for her. Speaks With Stars motioned for her to sit beside him as she approached. She sat down on the rocks, next to his fire, in the middle of her yard in Frederick, Colorado.

"What the hell is happening? Where is Bella?" Shanann hung her head as tears rolled in torrents down her cheeks. It was all too much. How had all of this happened? Her shoulders swayed back and forth as she sobbed. Her emotions drained into the earth, into the smell of sage, into the crackle of the fire, into the strength of the man who sat at her side. Shanann looked through her tears and was overwhelmed by the compassion she saw in his eyes. His gaze somehow calmed her. She looked off into space for a moment before she spoke through her tears.

"I couldn't save them. It was my job to protect them. I lost my mind over their allergies and their illnesses, and I couldn't keep them alive."

Speaks With Stars took looked directly into her tear-filled eyes.

"You are a good mother. Your children love you more than you know."

His words were comforting, yet Shanann was still filled with doubt. The only thing she knew for certain was that she needed to find Bella, to somehow make all of this okay. She wanted Gran. She wanted to take Bella into the light and the fragrance. She wanted to hold CeCe and Nico. She thought of the soft skin of her son and his newborn smell. She held her arms as if she were rocking him gently, back and forth, humming a lullaby. Speaks With Stars accompanied her soft voice with the flute, with the music of his people from a time of peace and contentment; a time long ago. But in this place, maybe it was yesterday. Speaks With Stars smiled and continued their song. Shanann fell asleep by the fire, lulled into a deep dream state with the vast beauty of the twinkling stars, the crackle of the fire, and Speaks With Stars' stable presence.

***

When Shanann woke up she was surprised to find herself in an old saloon right out of a Western movie. *Okay, now what?* The more she thought about it, the less surprised she was. Waking up in weird situations had almost become the norm. A man was sitting at the end of the bar on one of the stools. He was completely oblivious to her presence; even when he glanced her way, he seemed to look right through her. He reeked of alcohol and it sounded like he was justifying himself over something. The saloon was dusty and in need of a good cleaning. She wasn't going to volunteer. That was as old inclination. She was jolted from her random thoughts when the man started getting louder in his ranting. He was quite tall and large in stature. She immediately felt like he could be intimidating. She wasn't afraid of him, but had a sensation that he had been through one hell of an ordeal. She had the very odd sensation that many people had been terrified by his presence. He started to get louder and she could make out what he was saying, but was astonished by his words.

"Damn any man who sympathizes with Indians! I have come to kill Indians, and believe it is right and honorable to use any means under God's heaven ... Kill and scalp all, big and little; nits make lice!"

Oh my God, who is this guy? Much to her surprise, after his declaration, he began to weep. It was an awkward moment. Having spent so much time with Chris, she wasn't used to any outward emotion from a man. Snot was running down his face as he mumbled another incoherent statement and without warning, he fell off of his stool next to the bar. She took the moment to look more closely. She was the only one in the room with this strange man. He had on some kind of old uniform with two rows of buttons all the way down the front. He had a thick mustache and a beard. His hair was thinning and he looked like a character from the old Westerns she had seen as a kid. She was bending down near his face when he suddenly grabbed her by the arm. Shanann was so startled, she let out a little yelp that caught his attention. He turned his head to look at her and Shanann could not believe what she saw. The terror in his eyes was nothing she could have ever imagined. His gaze almost felt like it was burning her skin.

"Let me go, let me go," she insisted.

He looked right through her and began speaking. At first, she couldn't make out his words, but then they became clear, "The babies are screaming. Make them stop. Shoot them. Make them stop. They won't stop crying."

Struggling against his powerful grip, Shanann was able to yank herself from him. She stumbled back, trying to get out of his reach. He just kept repeating himself over and over. "The babies are crying. Make them stop."

She suddenly felt very sorry for this man. He was experiencing a grief that was unfathomable. She had never imagined such despair was possible. In a moment of complete defeat, he sunk back against the bar, hung his head and continued softly murmuring. For some reason, Shanann couldn't bear to leave him alone. She felt such pity. Finally, she could hear him snoring and felt comfortable enough to leave the saloon.

She began walking, having no idea where she was, or where she was going. She had a sense that it was okay and she would find her way back to where she belonged. Shanann smelled the sage before she saw his fire in her front yard. She walked up to Speaks With Stars and sat beside him. He offered her the pipe and she happily took it.

"You are feeling better?" he asked.

"Yes, much," she affirmed. "I confronted Chris. I don't know if he knew it was me, or if he thought he was facing his own conscience, but I feel better."

Speaks With Stars thought she sounded more like herself.

"I met a man in a saloon," Shanann revealed.

"Ah, you met the Colonel," Speaks With Stars explained.

"Who is he? I have never seen a person so overwhelmed with grief," Shanann expressed.

"He led the raid against my village. In order to make peace with the white man, my people were forced to live in a harsh land far away from the buffalo. We had to travel great distances to hunt, and the young men in the tribe grew wary of the men who took our land. They went out and raided the settlers and some people were killed. The Colonel and many men came into the village when the warriors were out hunting. The soldiers were drunk and thirsty for blood. They were not regular army and they had no discipline. We hung the white flag of peace, but they ignored the flag, and the treaty we had with their leaders. They slaughtered the women, the children, and the old people in our village without mercy. They took their bodies, dismembered them, and hung their parts on their horses. They had a parade in the town showing off the body parts of my people."

"Is that when you died?" Shanann asked, realizing what a bizarre question it was.

"My wife and I escaped. We were killed in a different battle, some years later."

"And Silver Moon, was this when she was murdered?" Shanann thought of the kind woman, with the hauntingly beautiful brown eyes, who had come to comfort her. Shanann had learned about the first settlers and how unfairly the Native Americans had been treated, but sitting here with this gentle man of peace and having met Silver Moon, such a gentle soul, made it all very personal. "I am so sorry. How can people be so cruel? They slaughtered the babies?"

"Yes, all of the children were killed. An honorable soldier who refused to take part in the slaughter gave an account of a small boy who was used as target practice, before he was killed."

"That poor little boy, he must have been terrified. Was the Colonel arrested?

"Some of the soldiers, those who refused to fight with him, spoke against him, but the courts did not hold him accountable," Speaks With Stars explained.

"The Colonel was pleading for the babies to stop crying. He was horrified by the sound of their cries," Shanann said with sadness and curiosity.

"Every morning, the Colonel gets up and preaches a sermon about righteousness and the superiority of the brave men and women who were settling the West. He speaks of his divine right to be here, to live on the land where my people have lived for many years. My people didn't understand this idea of ownership. We have a relationship with the water, the fire, and the sky. The earth is our mother. The buffalo and the deer blessed us, and we never took more than we needed. We thanked their spirits and felt gratitude. These people came, they took more than they needed, and they left us with nothing. That didn't make sense to my people. No one can own the land! We came to believe that the white men had a disease. Wetiko, a disease of the spirit. Those who take more than they can possibly use. My people felt bad for the men who were clearly ill. They were willing to share with them, teach them how to survive the long winters, so they would not starve to death. The Colonel, he was worse than most. He wanted all of my people dead. He wanted everything his own way. And now he cannot make the cries of the children go away. He is tormented, so he drinks until he passes out, until he cannot dream. I am sure the Colonel felt justified. He was disconnected from the children, from the women and the elders he killed. He did not think of them as human beings, just a problem that he needed to remove. I do not think he knew his actions would have such devastating consequences.

"I think the Colonel was a coward, just like my husband is a coward. Chris wasn't brave enough to ask me for a divorce. I guess he wanted us to just disappear. Maybe he had the disease of the spirit. What did you call it, wetiko? Chris and the Colonel both believed they had the right to take what wasn't theirs. How can someone be so disconnected?" Shanann sat pondering. A shiver ran down her spine. *Does Chris even feel emotions like other people? Was he born that way? Did something happen when he was a little boy? Did I make it worse?*

Speaks With Stars could feel Shanann's despair.

"You said that Chris gave everything freely, trying to be the best at everything so he would be seen as a good person. Maybe he did not know how to be himself and needed the spider-trickster to fit in," Speaks With Stars offered.

"Maybe Chris spent so much time pretending to be what he thought he should be, that when he tasted life without us, his mask fell off. He realized he wasn't really connected to us at all and getting rid of us wasn't that big of a deal." Shanann's voice was trembling as she spoke. "I am an adult, and what we did or didn't have in our marriage may have been part of his decision, but my children were innocent in all of this and what Chris did was..." Shanann couldn't speak the words. She was shaking with grief and anger. "I was a fool to ever believe him, and I let my children down. I let their father murder them."

Speaks With Stars knew this was far from the truth, but feared that his words were useless. He could feel the poison, the detachment, hovering over her as Shanann walked toward her house. He could smell ash and stench from the burnt structure. He did not want this young woman to lose herself in guilt and grief. He did not want her to walk in the regret and suffering like the Colonel and many others.

Shanann felt cold and alone, disconnected. *Was she a failure as a mother?* She suddenly had a thought that sent a chill down her spine. She turned and asked Speaks With Stars, "The Colonel, is he stuck here because of his crimes?" Shanann asked, not sure that she wanted to know the answer.

Speaks With Stars gently answered her question, "He believes that he is being punished, but he can leave this place anytime. There is only one person's forgiveness that he needs."

Chapter 11

Chris was ushered into the courtroom. He was dressed in prison orange pants and a short sleeved shirt. His hair was short and his close cut beard seemed unkept. He was wearing dark rimmed glasses that blocked a clear view of his eyes. His bottom lip was tucked in during much of the sentencing, as if trying to find a place to hide, an escape from this nightmare. His hands were cuffed and his ankles were shackled. It seemed like a short time ago, he had entered a different courtroom and pled guilty to all charges. His legal team had gone to D.A. Rourke and asked for a plea deal. Christopher Watts would plead guilty to all counts against him if they would not seek the death penalty. D.A Rourke immediately flew to North Carolina to speak with the Rzucek family. He needed to know what their feelings were. It didn't take long to understand that Shanann's family, especially Sandy, was adamantly against seeking the death penalty. When D.A. Rourke explained the details to her, she asked why he hadn't already accepted the plea deal, and that was his answer.

The Honorable Judge Kopcow began the proceedings as D.A. Rourke informed the court that the Rzucek's and the Watts' families were present, and they had been informed of their rights under the Victim's Rights Act. Judge Kopcow explained the procedures, and his expectations for conduct in the courtroom.

Chris sat silently, looking forward, not making eye contact with anyone until his father-in-law, Frank, stepped forward. Chris looked up at Frank for a brief moment, then lowered his gaze when his father-in-law began to speak.

"I would like to say to the court," Frank shivered briefly, paused, and took a step back. D.A. Rourke moved in close, as if to steady him. Frank continued, "Shanann, Bella, CeCe, and Nico were caring people. They loved life." It took everything Frank had to maintain his composure as he tried to steady his voice. He needed to make his statement. He needed to address his son-in-law, man to man. "They loved being around people who loved them. They always had good times. This is the first time they went to the beach and they loved it. God only knows what happened that night. Life will never be the same without Shanann, Bella, Celeste, and Nico." Frank braced himself, holding back the tears as he continued, "They had all of their lives to live. They were taken by a heartless one. This is the heartless one, the evil monster. How dare you take the lives of my daughter, Celeste, Bella and Nico! I trusted you to take care of them, not kill them. And they also trusted you, the heartless monster, and then you took them out, like trash. You disgust me. They were loving and caring people. You may have taken their bodies from me, but you will never take the love they had for me. They loved us more than you will ever know, because you don't know what love is. Because if you did, you would not have killed them. You monster, I don't know how you thought you could get away with this. The cameras do not lie. You carried them out of the house like trash. Yes, I've seen the videotape. You buried my daughter Shanann, and Nico, in a shallow grave. Then you put Bella and Celeste in huge containers of crude oil. You heartless monster. You have to live with this vision everyday of your life, and I hope you see this every time you close your eyes. Oh, I forgot you have no heart, or feelings, or love. Let me tell you something, I will think of them every day of my life, and I will love them every day of my life. Prison is too good for you. This is hard to say, but may God have mercy on your soul. I hope you enjoy your new life. It is nothing like the one you had out here. I hope the court shows you no mercy. It hurts every day.

It hurts in so many ways. I have heard people say you aren't a monster, no you are an evil monster. Love you Shanann, Bella, CeCe and Nico. Love you, Pop-pop. And one other thing, Shanann says she is super excited for justice today. Thank you, your Honor." Frank turned around, and faced Chris directly, for just an instant. Chris did not meet his gaze, but looked down into the nothingness as he bit his lip. Frank made his way back to his seat, shaken and desperately, holding back the tears, and the torment of this unthinkable moment.

District Attorney, Michael Rourke, read Frankie Rzucek's statement. Shanann's only sibling, the brother who idolized her, stood next to D.A. Rourke as his words went from the page to his brother-in-law's ears.

"Your Honor, the past three months I have barely slept. I have been going through a lot of different emotions and I did not see this coming. You went from being my brother, my sister's protector, one of the most loved people in my family, to someone I will spend the rest of my life trying to understand. What gave you the right to put your hands on a woman, let alone my best friend, my beloved sister, your daughter's and your son? Why weren't they enough for you? In the blink of an eye, you took away my whole world, people that mattered to me the most."

Frankie looked over his shoulder at Chris, looking for an answer to that question. Why? As D.A. Rourke continued to read off the page Frankie tried to maintain his emotions and not falter under the pressure of his shattered heart.

"They trusted you, they loved you. They looked up to you. You promised to keep them safe, instead you turned on your family. My blood is boiling as I write these last words, because they are the last ones you will ever hear from me. I can't even try to describe the betrayal and the hate I feel. And to be honest, you aren't even worth the time and effort it takes to put my pen to this paper. There isn't a day that goes by that I don't cry for my family. They were my whole world. All I do is ask myself why, why would you do this? You don't deserve to be called a man. What kind of person slaughters the people who loved them the most? Did you really think you would get away with this? Did you really think that this was your best option, to throw away your family like garbage? They deserve better and you know it. I hope you spend the rest of your life staring at the ceiling each night, haunted by what you have done. None of us deserve this. Hearing my mother and father cry themselves to sleep, in this hotel room, causes me anguish that is beyond words. I can't describe how this feels, how badly my heart is breaking for my poor parents. We trusted you. You have taken my family from this earth, but you can never take them from my heart. You took away my privilege of being an uncle to the most precious little girls I have ever known. I will never hear the words 'Uncle Frankie' again. But you will never be called dad again either. You will never be able to put your hands on another woman, let alone my best friend, my beloved sister and her son. I just can't comprehend how they weren't enough for you. Shanann, Bella, and CeCe loved you more than anyone. I pray that you never have a moment's peace, or a good night's rest. You will spend every day of your life in a cage, a cage you are privileged to live in, because my family isn't evil like you. We begged the district attorney to spare your life, because despite everything, we believe that no one has the right to take the life of another, even someone like you. I feel sorry for your family, the pain they must feel knowing they can't hug you, because that is what my mother, my father, and I feel every time we cry for our family. I wish that you would tell the truth, but I know that is more than you are capable of. My life will never be the same because of you, but at least my conscience is clear. I get to live freely, but I can't say the same for you.

My family and I can finally grieve after today. If anything, we will come out of this stronger than before, and we will continue to pray for your family. Sincerely, Frankie Rzucek."

Sandy Rzucek stepped up to the podium. She had on black pants and a black suit coat. A purple ribbon was pinned to her left shoulder in remembrance. The judge asked her to identify herself. "I am Sandy Rzucek, Shanann's mother. I wanted to say thank you for his moment. I want to take a moment to thank everyone who has prayed for our beloved family, who have sent gifts, and cards to us from all over the world. I know God will put the evil people where they need to be. I also want to take time to thank the town of Frederick, Greely, the D.A.s office, the FBI, and the CBI, for exceptional work. We thank Nickole Atkinson, and Shanann's neighbor Nathan and his family. To me, they are our heroes. They really are. God bless. God makes no mistakes on who he puts in your life. Marriage is about love, trust, friendship, and unity. We marry for sickness and health, till death do us part. Our daughter, Shanann, loved you with all of her heart. Your children loved you to the moon and back. Shanann's family was her world. Shanann put a crown on your head, but unfortunately the day that you took their lives, God removed that crown. We loved you like a son, we trusted you. Your faithful wife trusted you. Your children adored you, and they also trusted you." Sandy continued, her lip quivering as she held back the tears. "Your daughter, Bella Marie, sang a song proudly. I don't know if you were able to see the video, but she sang, 'daddy you're my hero'."

As Sandy continued, the thought of Bella singing that sweet song was too much. Sandy swallowed her tears, and her voice wavered in sorrow, "I don't know who gave you the right to take their lives, but I know God and his mighty angels, were there at that moment to bring them home to paradise. God gives us free will. So not only did you take the family of four, your family of four, you took your own life. I want the world to know that our daughter, and her children were so loved by us. They will always be protected by God, and his mighty angels. I didn't want death for you, because that's not my right. Your life is between you and God now, and I pray that he has mercy for you. As Shanann's mother, Bella Marie's, Celeste Kathrine's, and Nico Lee's, Nana. Thank you, Your Honor."

Judge Kopcow proceeded, asking if Cindy and Ronnie Watts wished to make a statement under the Victim's Rights Act. They stepped forward along with their representative. Cindy gazed at Chris as she passed by the desk he was sitting at. He looked down and did not return her eye contact.

The Judge asked them to introduce themselves to the court. In a very quiet voice, Cindy stated her name, and Ronnie did the same.

The Judge continued, I have authorized you to make a statement to the court as paternal grandparents of the children, and if you choose not to make a statement, but your designee chooses to do so, you may do that as well.

Miss Powers responded to the Judge, "They have written out their statements and hope they have the strength to speak, but if they do not, they would like for me to read them."

"That will be fine, who will be going first?"

Miss Powers responded, "If I could start Your Honor? On behalf of the Watts, Your Honor, and the community, we thank you for the opportunity and the recognition under the Victim Bill of Rights. We come today as the grandparents and the parent, of the daughter and children whose lives were taken in this case. We are not here to ask for leniency, and we are not here in any way condoning, or tolerating the crime that has occurred, and the pain that has been caused.

We join with our daughter-in-law and grandchildren's family, saying this should never have happened. This is something we will never get over. We appreciate the consideration from the family. We appreciate that they begged for Christopher's life. We agree and echo what they have said, that it was not his place take anyone's life, nor would it be our places, as a community, to take his life. We thank you for the opportunity, and for every consideration, and effort that has been put out. The prosecution in this case has, in fact, respected the Victim's Bill of Rights and explained that the information that my clients had at the time they were interviewed, was not correct. They were misinformed, and they were searching for answers, and they were not intending to cause pain to anyone. They appreciate that the prosecution answered the questions and gave them time, respect, and consideration so they could tell the court and everyone in this community that they accept that their son has done this. They accept that he chose to plead guilty, and the request for their consent and agreement to a life sentence.

Ronnie and Cindy Watts stood silently, each word spoken weighing heavily, adding to their agony.

Miss Powers continued, "They appreciate that he is given the opportunity to serve that life sentence. It is his responsibility and his sentence, and it is not enough to make up for what has been done. We understand and we join the family in that we have questions. We don't know how such a thing could have happened, or how a man responsible for raising his children, and protecting his wife, would take such actions. The steps that he took, disregarding their bodies, putting the community through the investigation, and discovery, and the responsibility of bringing justice; we do not understand that, and do not think it was appropriate, and we cannot begin to think that an explanation will every justify it. My clients indicate that they understand that a full opportunity for a confession, with all of the responsibility, and accountability, has not occurred. And they desire, if not today, at an appropriate time, and in an appropriate manner, an explanation, so that everyone can have peace, and come to understand, to the best of their ability, the details they need to have their questions answered. And by giving this opportunity of a life sentence, we hope that he embraces that moment. Had the death penalty been pursued, there would not have been an opportunity to be accountable, and to give a full confession. Had the death penalty been sought, he would have fought for his life, and the prosecutors would have been engaged in a multi-year battle. The families would have been torn apart. The financial cost and the emotional turmoil of a trial would have been devastating for the community. We have so much respect and gratefulness that did not happen. We would strongly encourage Christopher Watts to give that full confession in the tone and timing, he thinks appropriate, with the guidance of his council. We feel it would be helpful and appropriate to ease the pain and suffering, but we also say, we do not think there is anything that he can say that will ever account for his behavior. There is nothing that can be done to undo the harm he has caused. He has the responsibility to serve his sentence with dignity, and with regard to everyone, and to spend every breath he has left in atonement for what he has done."

Miss Powers finished the statement and stepped away from the podium so Cindy Watts, Chris's mother, could step forward. This was all a nightmare, but it was her time to speak, to finally let Chris know what she was feeling, and what was in her heart.

"My name is Cindy Watts. I am the grandmother of two beautiful granddaughters, Bella Marie, and Celeste Catherine Watts. I am also the mother of Christopher Watts, and I will be directing most of my statement to him. First, I would like to begin by recognizing the absolute horror of this crime, and acknowledging the devastating loss that the Rzucek family, and our family, have faced." Cindy continued to speak, her voice was shaking and she was holding back tears. Her husband stood silently by her side, his face, revealing a deep sadness that no words could express. Cindy composed herself and went on with her statement, "Our families have been irreparably broken by the needless deaths of Shanann, Bella, CeCe, and Nico. This is something we will never get over. We will always mourn the loss of our family, and in that, we are united in our grief. I am still struggling to understand how, and why, this tragedy occurred. I may never be able to understand and accept it, but I pray for peace, and healing for all of us. Now to my son Christopher."

Cindy's voice was shaking as she fought back tears, "I have known you since the day you were born, and you came into this world. I have watched you grow from a quiet, sweet, curious child, who Bella reminded me so much of, to a young man, who worked hard in sports, and later in mechanics to achieve your goals. You were a good friend, brother, father, and son. We have loved you from the beginning and we still love you. It might be hard for some to understand how I can sit here, under these circumstances, telling you we are heartbroken, that we cannot imagine what led us to this day, but we love you. Maybe you can't believe it either. As the Lord said in Jeremiah, 3:31, 'I have loved you with an everlasting love, therefore I have continued my faithfulness to you'. And, as your mother, Chris, I have always loved you and I still do. I hate what has happened. Your father, sister, and I are struggling to understand why, but we will remain faithful as your family, just as God remains faithful, because of his unconditional love for us all."

Cindy turned for the podium and looked directly at her son. Chris was holding back tears, but did not meet his mother's gaze. She continued in a broken voice, "We love you and we forgive you son!" Cindy wiped the tears from her eyes, took a deep breath, and stepped aside.

Miss Powers asked the Judge for permission to read a statement from Chris's dad.

"My name is Ronnie Watts, and I am the grandfather of Bella, Celeste and Nico, and I am the father of Shanann. I am the father of Christopher Watts, as well. One of the most important things I have done in my life, is to raise my children and to watch as they started their own families. I spent many years coaching little league, talking to my son, taking him to races, and sharing my love and knowledge of cars with him. He has been just as involved, with his own girls. I believe he loves his girls. I know he does. This tragedy has impacted my family in so many ways. Beyond losing our precious grandchildren, and our beloved daughter-in-law, we are forced to question everything. We still don't have all the answers, and I hope one day, Christopher, you can help us. Chris, I want to talk to you, as a father. Son, you are here today accepting responsibility, but I want to tell you this now, I love you. Nothing will ever change that. I want you to find peace, and today is your first step. The bible says, if we confess our sins, God is faithful, and just, and will forgive us. Chris, I forgive you, and your sister forgives you. We will never abandon you, and we love you, Dad."

The Judge proceeded to ask if there were any others, who had statements, under the Victim's Rights Act, that wished to speak. It was noted for the record, there were not. Judge Kopkow asked the defense attorney if he wished to present any evidence. He recorded that the defense had nothing to present. He asked the District Attorney if wished to make a statement. Chris had tears running down his cheeks as he looked around the courtroom. He wiped this face on his orange shirt, bit his lip, and braced himself for what he knew was coming.

D.A. Michael Rourke, stepped up to the podium. He had spent days agonizing over this crime. It was now his turn to speak, to express the story of Shanann, and her children. "Your Honor there are no words to adequately describe the unimaginable tragedy that brings us before this court today. By my comments, I'm not even going to try to express the horror, the pain, or the suffering that the defendant has caused to these families, to the community, and to all who are a part of this investigation. However, I do want to spend a few minutes sharing with the court, the details of the crime. So far, you have only had the opportunity to review the affidavit, and a few facts here and there, that have been offered to the court, in the motions, and the pleadings that have been filed. The questions that have screamed out to anyone who will listen, since August thirteenth, two-thousand-eight, why, and how? Why did this have to happen? How can a seemingly normal father, and a husband, annihilate his entire family, for what? These are the questions that only one individual in this courtroom, or on this planet, knows the answers to. I fully expect we will not receive the answers to these questions today, nor will we, at any time in the future. I don't expect that he will ever tell the truth about what truly happened, or why. Even if he did, there is no rational way any human being could find those answers acceptable responses to such horrific questions. The best we can do, is try to piece together some kind of understanding, from the evidence that is available to us. And the evidence tells us this, the defendant coldly, and deliberately ended four lives. Not in a fit of rage, not by way of accident, but in a calculated, and sickening manner."

D.A. Rourke took a deep breath. He pondered his own words as he spoke them. None of this made any sense. Everything had unfolded with such a speedy timeline, no one had time to process it. Chris had determined that he didn't want the families to go through a lengthy trial, so it was a wrap. There was no picking apart the many loose ends, or trying to put the pieces of a puzzle together, that did not fit. This would remain a mystery that everyone would wonder about for a long time.

Rourke continued, "Shanann was thirty-four years old. She had married the defendant in November, two-thousand-twelve. Over the weekend, leading up to August thirteenth, she had been at a work conference in Phoenix Arizona. She returned home in the early hours of August thirteenth. We know she got home about 1:45 in the morning. The doorbell camera, at their home, shows her arriving from the airport. Shortly thereafter, at least according to the defendant, they had, what he referred to, as an emotional conversation about the state of their marriage, and about what their lives would look like going forward. Whatever was said during that emotional conversation, only he knows. What we do know is, shortly after, the defendant strangled her to death with his own hands. We know that he slowly took her life, the morning of August thirteenth. We know that this was not done in an uncontrolled vengeful manner, as he tried to describe to agents from the CBI, and the FBI. If that were the case, you would expect to see vicious, horrible bruising about her neck, shoulders and face. You would expect to see the hyoid bone in her neck broken. You would expect to see some kind of defensive wounds on his body, as she struggled, and fought for her own life. None of those are present. The only injury on Shanann's body, was one set of bruising that appeared to be fingernail, or finger mark, bruising to the right side of her neck. We know, our experts tell us, that it takes two to four minutes to strangle someone to death manually, with their own hands. The horror that she felt when the man that she loved, wrapped his fingers around her throat, and choked the life out of her, must have been unimaginable. Even worse, what must Bella, age four, and Celeste, age three, must have thought when their father, the one man on this planet who was supposed to nurture and protect them, snuffed out their lives? They both died from smothering. Let me say that again, the man seated to my right, smothered his daughters. Why? Imagine the horror in Bella's mind, as her father took her last breath away. Your Honor, I understand very clearly Bella fought for her life. The frenulum, the connective tissue between her upper lip, and her gum, had a centimeter and a half laceration. She bite her tongue multiple times before she died."

Chris sat at the desk just behind the D.A. He hung his head, his eyes were closed, and his face reflected shame, and anguish. Chris took deep breaths, as if he were trying to hold back tears.

D.A. Rourke continued, "She fought for her life, as her father smothered her. Celeste had no such injuries. In fact she had no external injuries at all. But according to the medical examiner, she was smothered nonetheless. The defendant then methodically, and calmly, loaded their bodies into his work truck. Not in a hasty, disorganized way. He was seen from the neighbor's doorbell camera backing his truck into the driveway, going back and forth, into the house, and back out to the truck, three different times. One time for each of their bodies.

Chris sat very still, listening, trapped. He was handcuffed, shackled, and he could feel every eye in the building burning a hole through him. They did not see the good guy he had always been. D.A. Rourke's description of what happened, shot through him like a knife. Chris knew it was not entirely accurate. What would everyone think if they knew the real story?

Shanann was face down on the bed only moments after he had strangled her, when Bella came into the room.

"What's wrong with mommy?" Bella had asked.

"Mommy doesn't feel good," Chris responded.

He was shocked to see Bella. *I thought Bella was... How did she wake up?* This was the nightmare he had attempted to avoid. He wrapped Shanann in the bed sheet, and tried to carry her down the stairs. She was too heavy, he dropped her, and she slid down the stairs with a heavy thump, at the bottom. CeCe heard the noise, and sleepily joined her sister. The girls were confused and Bella started crying. He gathered what he needed for work, made himself a lunch, and carried Shanann out to the truck. He put her on the floor of the back seat, her head and feet covered in black plastic bags, so the girls wouldn't have to see her. He took his daughters, in their jammies, with their 'binkies', and sat them in the back seat of his truck. The trip to the oil site was about forty-five minutes. Chris's thoughts were interrupted and he was back in the room.

D.A. Rourke continued, "Chris then drove them away from their family home, one final time, intending to hide any evidence of the crimes he had just committed. In one final act of callousness towards his wife, his daughters, their unborn son, he took their remains, and drove them to a location where he thought no one would ever find them, to the oil tank batteries he was so familiar with. He knew this was safe. He had texted a co-worker the night before saying, 'I'll head out to that site. I'll take care of it.' He had carefully ensured that he would be alone in the middle of the plains, where he could secure away the remains of his family, a place he hoped they would never be found. In one final measure of disrespect for the family he once had, he ensured they would not be together, even in death, or so he thought. He deposed of them in different locations. He buried

Shanann and Nico in a shallow grave, away from the oil tanks."

Everyone in the courtroom sat in the heavy silence of disbelief, and unimaginable sorrow. Chris drifted off into memory. *What had actually happened? Couldn't I have saved my girls? Couldn't I have done something? Why did I do that? I don't know! This is my flesh and blood, I wanted to be a dad all my life, just to have kids. And they love me, nothing makes sense.* He had pulled up to Cervi 319. The girls were scared, sitting in the back seat of the truck, huddling together, leaning on one another, occasionally drifting off to sleep. Other moments they were crying softly. During the entire trip, they never let go of one another. Chris stopped the truck and got out. He pulled Shanann out of the truck and started digging a hole with his work shovel. The girls didn't know what was going on. CeCe started to cry. He opened the back door, took CeCe's blue Yankees blanket, covered her tiny mouth, and smothered her. He knew Bella was watching as he carried CeCe's body up the ladder, opened the eight inch hatch, and dropped her in the oil tank. When he got back to the truck, Bella asked, "Are you going to do to me what you did to CeCe?" Her small, frail voice rang in his ears, as he took the same blanket, and covered Bella's face. "No daddy, no." Bella fought back. She had just seen her sister smothered and thrown away. She knew her mommy and her brother were in the dirt next to the truck.

D.A. Rourke continued, "Bella and Celeste were thrown away in different oil tanks at this facility, different tanks, so they wouldn't be together in death. Imagine this Your Honor, the defendant took these little girls, and put them through a hatch at the top of an oil tank, eight inches in diameter." Rourke rounded his hands to show the judge the size of the small space he was describing. "Bella had scratches on her left buttocks, from being shoved through this hole. A tuft of blonde hair was found on the edge of one of these hatches. The defendant told investigators that Bella's tank seemed emptier than CeCe's, because of the sound that the splashes made. These were his daughters. Significantly, his co-workers arrived at the tank battery later that morning, and they all described him as perfectly normal. It was a normal work day. Even while his daughter's sank in oil, and water, not far away from him. And then his efforts at deception truly began. We've all seen the emotionless interviews that the defendant gave to the local media, asking for help in locating his family. We've watched, as he claimed the house was empty without them, and he hoped they were somewhere safe, and he just wanted them to come home. He told investigators they were at home sleeping when he left for work that morning, and that Shanann had told him she was taking the girls to a friend's house for the day. What is striking about this case your Honor, beyond the horrors that I've already described to you, is the number of collateral victims that he created by his actions. While he stood in front of TV cameras, asking for the return of his family, scores of law enforcement officers, neighbors, friends and family scoured the area, fretting for their safe return. They texted him, begging for any information, and sending him their best wishes. All the while, he hid what he had done. The list of indirect victims doesn't not end there. Think of the firefighters, and the Colorado State Patrol Hazmat experts, who had to don protective suits, and who were called upon to pull Bella and Celeste out of those oil tanks. Or the coroners, who had to conduct these autopsies. Or the victim assistants, who frantically attempted to ease the suffering of those affected. All of this Your Honor, for what? Why? Why did this have to happen? His motive was simple Your Honor." D.A. Rourke paused and then continued, "He had a desire for a fresh start. To begin a relationship, with a new love, overpowering all decency, and feelings for his wife, his daughters and unborn son. While Shanann texted the defendant, over and over again, in the days and weeks leading up to her death, attempting to save her marriage, the defendant hid pictures of his girlfriend in his phone, and texted her at all hours of the night. While Shanann sent the defendant, self-help and relationship counseling books, one of which was, ironically, thrown in the garbage, he was searching the internet for secluded vacation spots to take his new love, and researching jewelry. And while Shanann took the girls to visit family in North Carolina, the defendant was visiting car museums, and the Sand Dunes, with his new girlfriend. The stark contrast between the subject's internet and text content, is absolutely stunning. Even after the morning he killed them, and disposed of their bodies, he made several phone calls. One call was to the school, where the girls were supposed to start, informing them that the girls would not be attending anymore. They were being un-enrolled, presumably to give him some more time before law enforcement were notified about them going missing. He contacted a realtor, and had a conversation about selling his house. He texted his girlfriend about their future. None of this answers the questions of why, however. If he was this unhappy and wanted a new start, why not get a divorce? You don't annihilate your family and throw them away like garbage." D.A. Rourke was filled with confusion as he continued his statement, "Why did Nico, Celeste, Bella and Shanann have to lose their lives in order for him to get what he wanted? Your Honor, justice demands the maximum sentence under the plea agreement reached by the parties. As you will recall the agreement calls for life sentences as to Shanann, Bella and Celeste, and all of those running consecutively to one another. It also calls for one count of unlawful termination of a pregnancy, as to Nico, to run consecutively with counts of one, two, and three. I would suggest that the extreme aggravation present in the defendant's conduct, and the efforts that I have described, mandates that counts seven, eight and nine, tampering with a deceased human body, each, the maximum of twelve years and that those sentences run consecutively to one another. It is very clear that these were not the subject of one act, but each oil tank that he walked up to, with his daughter's bodies, and the hole that he dug for his wife and unborn son, mandate a mandatory consecutive sentence. It has been alluded to this morning that the defendant was certainly eligible for the death penalty in this case, under the existing law in the state of Colorado. As you heard, Shanann's family strongly opposed my office seeking the death penalty, and being bound to the criminal justice system for the next several decades. That is, in large part, why we have reached the agreement that we have. Four lives were lost at the hands of the defendant on August thirteenth, for reasons that we will never fully understand, nor will we know. In the end, the Rzucek family was much more merciful towards him than he was towards his wife, his daughters, and his unborn son. Being in prison, for the remainder of his life, is exactly where he belongs for murdering his entire family. Thank you."

The Judge calmly and deliberately spoke to the court, "So the court has considered the arguments made by the attorneys. The court has considered the statements made by the victims in this case. The court is going to find that the plea agreement is fair and reasonable under the circumstances. I want to acknowledge the Rzucek and the Watts families, showing that mercy on Mr. Watts is understood, and I respect the decision to request the District Attorney not seek the death penalty in this case. This Court is going to accept the plea bargain, under the circumstances. The words that come to mind, when I hear the evidence in this case, are a senseless crime, and a viciousness of the crime. And equally aggravating, in this court's determination, is the despicable act of disposing of the bodies in the manner in which they were done in this case. I have been a judicial officer now, starting my seventeenth year, and I could objectively say, this is perhaps the most inhumane, and vicious case that I have handled, out of the thousands of cases I have seen. And nothing less than a maximum sentence would be appropriate, and anything less than the maximum sentence would depreciate the seriousness of this offense. So the court is going to sentence Mr. Watts as follows: With regard to count number one, murder in the first degree as it relates to Shanann Watts, the court is going to sentence you, sir, to a life sentence in the Colorado Department of Corrections, with no possibility of parole. And that is going to run consecutively."

The judge continued with the details of the sentence. Chris sat silently. Life with no possibility of parole were the only words he actually heard. He had pled guilty. It was his own choice, but the gravity of those words were closing in on him. His beautiful family was gone forever. His relationship with Nikki was over. He was in a nightmare of his own making, and his world was upside down, inside out, and backwards.

An overwhelming sadness filled the court room. There was no satisfaction, or feeling of vindication for the Rzucek family, only an earth shattering loss. Frank sat silently, dazed by the surreal moment. Having spent a torrent of tears earlier, he was emotionally drained. Sandy and Frankie leaned their heads together. Frankie would never hear the kids call him uncle, and the sister he adored and admired for so long would never hug him again. Sandy's tears and the sorrow that saturated her entire being, was palpable. She had lost her beloved daughter, three beautiful grandchildren and Chris, a son-in-law she still loved, despite the horror he had inflicted on the best parts of herself.

Chapter 12

The sentencing had been devastating. Shanann had seen her husband hand- cuffed, shackled and dressed in prison orange. That was his reality now. She saw her in-laws and her precious family, all devastated by the tragic outcome of Chris's actions. Shannann needed the earth mother. She closed her eyes and was suddenly standing on the cliff, Speaks With Stars' favorite place. The sun was setting and the view took her breath away. Pink and purple splashes, mingled with scattered flecks of gold filtering through soft wisps of blue, weaving in between hazy billows of fluff. Mountain peaks reached up to meet the lofty canvas of color and translucent light. A gentle breeze lifted the scent of pine and wild roses. Shanann reached her arms up towards the magnificent sky. This place, this gift, the mother, calmed her soul. Shannan's emotions were calmed, as she thought deeply about what had occurred. She could not imagine that her marriage, her beautiful children, the life she and Chris had built together, was so terrible that Chris needed to destroy it. She loved that man for a very long time. She believed that he had loved her. She could not have been wrong about everything. Her entire marriage was not a lie, she knew it. She didn't believe that her husband was evil, even though she couldn't think of an act more evil than the one he had committed against her and their children. She suddenly remembered what Speaks With Stars had said about the young men in his tribe, those disconnected from themselves. Thinking back, she knew there were times when Chris seemed unable to feel emotion. What had happened to her husband that had split him from

233

himself, that allowed him to turn off his emotions? Was it biological or chemical? Did he experience some kind of trauma? She knew all of her speculation was just that, speculation. She did not fully understand Chris's truth. As she pondered all of the ideas that bombarded her mind, she felt that she was not the only one speculating. She could hear rumblings of gossip, and assumption, and explicit hatred against her husband and oddly enough against herself. She thought of Inktomi, the spider-trickster, and the lies that had stolen Speaks With Stars' land, and ultimately led to the slaughter of his people. She could hear voices embracing the silence with doubt, and assertions of what might have occurred, regarding her murder. People made up their minds, without knowledge, without truth, without evidence. She found the idle accusations against her husband, and herself, oddly curious. She was filled with sorrow, knowing that unsubstantiated belief caused enormous pain for her parents, brother and friends. She knew, however, that everyone caught in Inktomi's world-wide-web of distractions would ultimately face the choices and the opinions they embraced. She felt compassion for those who judged her. Everyone was walking in their own experience and had reasons for what they chose to believe, yet no one could escape the mirror of their own truth, and everyone had to face the intended and unintended consequences of their own actions. Shanann closed her eyes, soaking up the gentle breeze, and suddenly found herself standing back in Frederick, Colorado in front of her house. She was startled by what she saw. The entire lawn was filled with beautiful flowers, candles, plants, wide eyed stuffed animals, brightly colored balloons, and messages of love and kindness. She was overwhelmed! So many people had come to her house, to show her and the children love and sympathy. She could feel the intention of all who had come, those who left gifts and expressed heartfelt emotion. She sensed their tears and deep sadness for her, Bella, CeCe and Nico. Shanann was overwhelmed with gratitude, and felt a joyful connection that was beyond soothing, a unity that was liberating. This was what she had been searching for. In a moment of perfect clarity, Shanann fully acknowledged her truth. She was filled with love, not regret. Shanann suddenly felt an overwhelming need to be close to her family.

***

The room was familiar. She sat by her parent's bed for what seemed like a very long time. Pop-pop was lightly snoring, and she was deeply comforted by the sight of him. Her mother looked beautiful and peaceful. Watching her mother sleeping, Shanann knew that her girls had been here. They had come to Sandy, who was dreaming about the experience.

"Hiya Nana!" CeCe was holding her little hands on both sides of Sandy's face and kissing her all over, and Sandy smiled as she slept. "You've been always so good to us Nana and we love you with our soul."

Shanann could hear Bella's voice, "Hi Nana, guess what? I can go to Disneyland any time I want now."

"That's right Bella, you can," Sandy whispered the words in her sleep.

"I love you, and Pop-pop, and Uncle Frankie," Bella's sweet voice declared.

Like a wisp, the dream ended, but Shanann knew the girls had deeply touched her mother's soul and Sandy was assured that they were safe and happy. Shanann reached down and whispered, "I love you mommy, and I'm sorry." She climbed in bed between her mom and dad. She closed her eyes and rested. After a moment, or a lifetime, she received the most precious gift. She saw herself through her parent's, and her brother's, eyes. The unconditional love poured into her being. They loved her like she loved Bella, CeCe and Nico. She had always known it, but to feel all of it at once, years of their love, was overwhelming. She felt whole and blessed and she couldn't wait to hold her babies. When she left her parents, she took a peek into Frankie's room, and she knew, without a shadow of a doubt, they would all be together again.

Chapter 13

Shanann walked up to her front lawn. He was waiting for her, like he always was.

"You look comforted my young friend," Speaks With Stars commented.

"I went home. Not to my house, but to my family. They love me so much, as much as I love Bella, CeCe and Nico.

Speaks With Stars smiled. He could see that she had found what she was looking for, and he knew it was time. Shanann suddenly heard a noise coming from inside the house. She stood up, and for the first time she asked Speaks With Stars if he would join her in the house. He agreed, and they both walked through the front door. All of her beautiful things were there, in the right place, but she barely noticed. All she could hear were the voices coming from the back yard. Shanann ran to the kitchen and opened the sliding glass door. She was stunned by what she saw. There were endless green meadows, flowers of every imaginable color. She could hear the exuberance of a bubbling brook, and the wind dancing in the trees, but the sound of children laughing was the sweetest thing she had ever heard. It was beyond description. She saw a little girl standing across the lawn and for a second she thought it was her Bella. The little girl had short hair, like someone had given her a haircut with a steak knife. She was in an oversized shirt with gray and blue stripes, held together with two big buttons. When the child turned, Shanann saw the largest, most beautiful blue eyes. She had one tiny blue barrette clinging to her short hair. That was when Shanann saw a small pair of hands coming from behind the bush the two girls were standing by. The little girl stepped toward her playmate and Shanann saw her Bella. She ran to her, scooped her up, and kissed her sweet face, over and over. Bella wrapped her arms tightly around Shanann's neck like she had done so many times.

"Oh, my girl, I am so happy to see you. I've been waiting for you."

Bella looked into Shanann's eyes, "No mama, I've been waiting for you."

Shanann felt a tug on her dress. CeCe and Nico were standing by her side. CeCe's beautiful smile and wild spirit was intensified in this place. She held so much joy. Her beautiful son stood by his sister. Nico's dark brown eyes, looking up at his mommy, melted Shanann's heart. She plopped down in the grass and all three of her children climbed into her lap. Hugs and kisses and sweet words reunited Shanann with her babies. Such joy was beyond anything she had ever imagined. Shanann was content to stay sitting in the grass with her children for an eternity, but they had other plans.

"Mommy we are going to pick some flowers," Bella stated.

CeCe chimed in, "I want to pick flowers. Come on, Nico."

Shanann wasn't sure she wanted to let her children out of her sight for even one second. She started to tell them to stay close, but she knew they would never be far from her again. At that moment the little girl with the amazing blue eyes walked up.

Bella walked over to the little girl and wrapped her arm around her playmate's waist. "This is my friend Lena, mommy."

Shanann reached down and took the little girl's hand, "Very nice to meet you, Lena," Shanann replied lovingly. Lena softly said something that Shanann didn't understand.

Shanann was surprised when her Bella jumped in to interpret for her, "She thinks you are beautiful," Bella stated.

"Thank you," Shanann replied, stunned by the whole scene.

Lena smiled. The two little girls locked arms and as they walked off to pick flowers Shanann saw numbers on the little girl's forearm. They skipped off with CeCe and Nico close behind. She looked at Speaks With Stars, "Is that what I think it is?"

"Yes, this child was in a Nazi prison camp, Auschwitz," he explained.

"And she is still here?" Shanann was aghast at the possibility.

"No, she just arrived, like your Bella," Speaks With Stars offered.

"What language was she speaking? I didn't understand her."

"She was speaking Polish, the language of her family," he explained.

"Why is she still wearing...?" Shanann didn't even want to speak of the horrors this child must have endured.

Speaks With Stars smiled, "She does not feel a need to dress like the other children. Her appearance is a reminder of the lessons she learned in the camps, of the great sacrifices she endured. This child acknowledges the atrocities humans are capable of. She is a Hope-giver. She symbolically holds the numbers, the butchered hair and the stripped shirt in remembrance, in hope of a more evolved future. Lena believes that people will act with greater understanding and kindness for one another. She believes the sacrifices of those in the Holocaust were not in vain. Everyone who meets her feels her conviction."

"I felt it when she touched my hand." Shanann paused before she continued, "This is all so confusing. How can Bella understand her language, and what do you mean Lena just arrived?"

"Look around you," Speaks With Stars encouraged.

Shanann looked across the beautiful plush lawn. The green seemed to go on forever. Small children of every nationality, all speaking their own native languages were running and playing together. There was no language barrier. They all understood one another perfectly.

"How can this be?" She was stunned by the beauty of the moment.

"Some of these children are like your Bella. They died tragically in unexpected deaths, and they came to this place to wait for their parents. Some of them just like to run and play. They are filled with light and love. They are full of joy and peace because they are all connected. They do not feel a language or a race barrier. They do not judge. There is only acceptance and curiosity for them. Waiting here is not agonizing. There is no sense that time has passed. There is only now. The clarity of the moment is enough."

Shanann took a deep breath. "Ah, why do the grownups experience torment before we get to come here and pick flowers?" Shanann asked jokingly.

Speaks With Stars smiled as he answered, "You could have come here at any time, but you were attached to your story, to your physical life. Your mind was not ready to accept what had happened to you. I think you wanted to understand why you left the physical world unexpectedly, at the hands of someone you trusted."

"My children died horrific deaths at the hands of their own father. I am so thankful they came directly here, but…"

"Children are not attached to the physical world the way you and I were. Their father treated them well every day of their lives, except one. The little ones are much closer to source. They can more readily accept what has occurred, because they have not been influenced by the world in the same way. They understand that that there is no room for guilt, shame, or anger in this place." He continued, "You said yourself that you and Chris were regimented, you had a way of doing things. Those patterns, dig deep grooves inside of your mind and they are hard to let go of. That is why the Colonel does the same thing over and over. His grooves are deeply implanted, seared into his being because they caused so much pain for his victims and himself."

She sat silently as she pondered the words of her dear friend. An understanding suddenly filled her being and everything became crystal clear. Bella had been waiting patiently for her. She instinctively knew Shanann needed to process her experiences. That was why Bella didn't reveal herself. Tears filled her eyes as she thought about her daughter's love and wisdom. Shanann looked across the lawn, at all of the delightful children laughing, hugging and playing. Silver Moon was standing in the middle of a group of what looked like Syrian, Kurdish, Native American, African, Vietnamese, Mexican and so many other children, all playing together. She was holding a beautiful young child in her arms. She looked at Shanann and smiled. The two women understood one another. Shanann reached down and touched the bracelet Silver Moon had given her. She was suddenly bursting with excitement as she turned to Speaks With Stars, "Gran is here, I can feel her." She looked at Speaks With Stars in astonishment, "My kids and Gran have been here the entire time." Shanann suddenly remembered the words Speaks With Stars had said to her when they were discussing Silver Moon, "When people are so filled with love, they are the light."

Shanann was stunned by the simplicity. "We don't go into the light at all, do we? The light comes into us, when we are ready to accept it."

Speaks With Stars smiled, "Judgement of others, and of oneself, diminishes the light. Acceptance strengthens it."

Shanann now fully understood the meaning of those words. She looked at this man who meant the world to her. "You aren't staying here, are you?"

"No, my path is by the fire. There are wondering souls who believe they are alone."

"Will everyone come to understand?" Shanann asked.

"Yes of course. They have eternity to figure it out."

"Will I see you again?" Shanann asked.

"Whenever you wish. Come, sit by the fire, and we will smoke a pipe together."

Speak with Stars walked away slowly. He returned to his quiet little fire, sat deliberately, and lit his pipe. "It is a good day," he declared.

Bella, CeCe, and Nico ran up, excited to present their mommy with a bouquet of wildflowers. Shanann thanked them before she picked up Nico and held him tightly. She remembered when she first saw him in Gran's arms; the sound of his cry and the softness of his skin. "My beautiful boy!" Shanann looked up and saw that Gran was waiting for them in the middle of the green flowing meadow. Bella took Shanann's hand and CeCe ran ahead as they all walked toward Gran. Shanann had never seen such a beautiful sky. An intense light burst through the orange and yellow concentration of clouds. A dark outline of trees could be seen as if their branches waved hello in the gentle breeze. Hues of blue and lavender filtered through the wisps of clouds, balancing the intense blaze of color with a balmy calm. The fragrance of flowers danced in the air. A peace filled Shanann's entire being, as she heard Bella's sweet voice softly singing, "You are my sunshine, my only sunshine, love you mama."

"Love you more," Shanann whispered.

Epilogue

I open the window shade, or take in some fresh air on the back porch. Next door, the Watt's backyard is silent. There is no life, nothing is cooking on the grill, the grass is brown and tumbleweeds line the foundation of the house. The swing looks lonely to me. I remember the giggles of the girls when they were playing. Looking at the house now, many see evil, or a haunted space. Many project their fears, and the horror of this despicable crime, onto the house.

I know that Shanann, Bella, CeCe and Nico, are not trapped in a dead house. They have moved on. The images that come to me now, are comforting and exciting. I can see the meadows where the children are laughing and playing. I can smell the intoxicating fragrance of flowers, or the comforting scent of sage. I can hear the soft sound of drumming and chanting.

I am convinced that we all go on, we are all connected. With an open heart, we can all hear our loved ones from another realm. I have studied many cultures, religions, and traditions. New scientific research shows that humans are predisposed to believe in an afterlife. While many pay homage and feel connected to their ancestors, there are those who actually have conversations, seek advice, and share a good joke with friends, and family, who are in another dimension. While many beliefs and traditions are centuries old, the scientific, cutting edge study of quantum physics reminds us, as humans, we still have much to learn. In my opinion, the only false narrative is the claim that anything is absolute. There is always another side, another aspect, a deeper understanding.

Given that the laws of nature are quite different from what we understand in the third dimension, I think we can all be confident that Shanann's entire transitional, journey probably occurred in the blink of an eye.

Printed in Great Britain
by Amazon